BOUND BY REVENGE

SINGHAM BLOODLINES BOOK 1

M V KASI & P. G. VAN

Contents

1. Chapter 1 — 1
2. Chapter 2 — 3
3. Chapter 3 — 8
4. Chapter 4 — 12
5. Chapter 5 — 15
6. Chapter 6 — 18
7. Chapter 7 — 22
8. Chapter 8 — 27
9. Chapter 9 — 29
10. Chapter 10 — 33
11. Chapter 11 — 37
12. Chapter 12 — 41
13. Chapter 13 — 44
14. Chapter 14 — 49
15. Chapter 15 — 52
16. Chapter 16 — 60
17. Chapter 17 — 65
18. Chapter 18 — 69
19. Chapter 19 — 72
20. Chapter 20 — 76
21. Chapter 21 — 83
22. Chapter 22 — 88
23. Chapter 23 — 92
24. Chapter 24 — 97
25. Chapter 25 — 103
26. Chapter 26 — 108
27. Chapter 27 — 115
28. Chapter 28 — 119

Contents

29. Chapter 29   129

30. Chapter 30   134

31. Chapter 31   139

32. Chapter 32   141

33. Chapter 33   150

34. Chapter 34   152

35. Chapter 35   156

36. Chapter 36   162

37. Chapter 37   165

38. Chapter 38   167

39. Chapter 39   174

CHAPTER ONE

"Turn around and look at me." The order was thrown in a chillingly calm tone.

Trembling and worried about the consequences, Anika slowly turned, and raised her eyes towards the man in front of her. Her vision was still blurry from her tears. She wiped them away and was met with the sight of the broad back of a tall man. He was turned away from her as he closed the door shut. Stepping back, she wrapped her arms around her protectively. She kept her wary eyes trained on his back, waiting for what, she didn't know.

As soon as he turned, she felt like the air around them was sucked away, making her gasp out loud. The man looked larger than life, and more importantly, he looked like he could easily kill her with a single blow.

Under the large skylight, the man didn't look like a monster at first glance—far from it. He was elegantly dressed and also good-looking with perfectly chiseled features. He also appeared to be close to her age.

His eyes scanned the mess she had made in the room, before he turned to look at her face dispassionately. She expected to see anger, but there was none.

He didn't say anything for a long moment, just kept his eyes firmly locked on her face.

After an indeterminate amount of time, he broke the deafening silence. "So. *You* are my bride-to-be," he stated rather than ask in a deep voice.

The word 'bride' broke through her trance and made adrenaline course through her body.

God, this is so messed up. Why am I cowering in fear?

She knew she cannot and should not give up her fight because of brute force. She was a problem solver, a logical thinker who had succeeded most of her life convincing people to think from her perspective. She should be able to use reasoning to invoke some compassion from the man whom she was supposed to marry.

"I don't want this," she whispered, unable to work up a louder voice. She kept her eyes on his face, pleading. "Please stop this marriage."

He didn't respond, and neither did he react.

"I don't want this wedding," she repeated. "We can think of another solution. We should be able to come up with a reasonable..." her voice trailed off when she saw him compressing his lips into a thin, hard line as he began to walk towards her.

Her pulse sped up beating wildly against her throat. Her heart began to pound hard in her chest until it ached. She wanted to scream and run away in fear, but she held her ground and kept her eyes on him.

Through trembling lips, she spoke again. "I'm not from your world. I don't belong here. Let me go back to my family," she reasoned.

As she spoke, she was close to being thrown back into a state of shock, reminding her once again that she was living a nightmare. She stood on a land of no rules, humanity, or compassion.

The man stopped in front of her until he was too close for comfort. She had to raise her eyes to look at him. As soon as she met his gaze, she flinched at the look he was directing towards her.

His eyes were riveted on her face as his mouth stretched into a sneer full of hate. "We are getting married *because* your precious family has begged me to do so. So, if you or your fucking family try to pull any stunt during our wedding today, and try to back out, I'm not going to spare anyone." He spat out the words 'your family' like they were a curse.

Slowly and deliberately his eyes swept over her body clothed in traditional bridal attire. "Nothing and no one—including you—can stop this from happening. You will become my wife by tonight," he vowed.

Listening to those words, her legs gave out from under her, and she collapsed on her knees, unable to swallow the defeat.

How could she let herself be trapped in this hellhole? Because of her one impulsive decision, she was going to lose everything.

CHAPTER TWO

Three days ago...

"Let's go, Ann, I'm starving."

A man's voice sliced through Anika's concentration.

"Is it lunch time already?" she asked, her voice husky for not having spoken for the past few hours. She had spent the entire morning updating her patient files, so another doctor on her team could continue when she was away on her vacation.

Nathan grinned next to her as she groaned and wiggled her stiff fingers. "Yup. It's close to two. They are going to close the cafeteria soon," he said as he moved behind her chair. The chair was supposed to be ergonomic, but it didn't help much, because her back felt stiff as hell.

She sighed as Nathan massaged her shoulders. "You know you could have avoided all this typing, Dr. Patel. Maybe you should rethink this impromptu vacation or at least postpone it."

She groaned as he loosened some of the tensed muscles. "Nice try, Dr. Smith. Stop sounding like my mom."

"You know Dr. Patel is right. She's not thrilled you are going to meet your so called family who didn't bother to get in touch with her after your dad passed away in an accident."

"Nathan, please. I've been through this already with Mom. I have made up my mind to go."

"Well, then at least change your mind about letting me tag along with you."

"You know I can't let you go with me, Nathan," she said gently.

He sighed. "I know."

There was an awkward silence between them. She knew Nathan was thinking about his proposal, and more importantly how she had turned him down.

Nathan was her best friend. They grew up together in the same neighborhood, attending the same schools, and also the same colleges. They even worked for the same hospital.

Apart from Nathan, she only had few other friends during college with whom she eventually grew apart when they began to work in a stressful career as a doctor.

It wasn't like she hated having friends or anything. She just wasn't used to making friends easily.

Until she had turned twelve, she had a stuttering problem. Most of the kids in her school and neighborhood either made fun of her speech problem or pitied her because of it. Even when she ultimately overcame her disability, the feeling of being shunned by her peers remained. Nathan was the only person who had treated her normally and as a friend.

Nathan was a serial dater who always had a line of women who came and went from his life. She had met and socialized with a few of his girlfriends, but none of them seemed to catch Nathan's attention for long. It came as a total surprise when Nathan had proposed to her one evening, after having invited her for an elaborate dinner he had planned at a rooftop restaurant.

"I love you, Dr. Anika Patel. Will you marry me?"

She was stunned as they had not been on a date before that night. "Nathan... I-I... can't. I can't marry you."

His face fell.

"I love you, Nathan. But...not like that."

He nodded and forced out a smile. "I know. I just thought it would be funny to see how you'd react."

They had both known it wasn't a joke. They tried getting back to their casual friendship, but that night stayed in their minds. Since then, she made it a point not to encourage Nathan in anyway, because she didn't want to disappoint him again.

"Dammit! Let's go! They are going to close the café soon." Nathan looked at his watch hurrying out.

She grabbed her bag and followed him.

"So what do you feel like eating today?" he asked as they approached the large cafeteria that was mostly empty as it was almost closing time.

"The sushi counter is open. Let's grab that."

They paid for their food and sat down next to a large picture window overlooking the Bay Bridge.

"Oh great," Nathan grumbled, as they began to eat.

"What?"

"It's that creepy guy. And he's at it again, staring at you."

"Huh?" Anika twisted her body slightly and looked at the large guy behind one of the cafeteria counters. Turning back, she shook her head in amusement.

"It's not funny, Ann. The guy keeps turning up at most places we go. You should let me deal with him."

"You are over thinking this, Nathan. He's just some random dude who's working here, and also pulling in shifts at the coffee house and other places around here. We just happened to go to those places, too. It's called a *coincidence.*"

Nathan grumbled. "Maybe, but him staring at you so much is not a coincidence."

"Are you saying that a guy staring at me is odd?" she asked in a mock outraged tone.

Nathan grinned. "No. A guy staring at you, and not doing anything about it—is odd. Guys keep hitting on you all the time."

Yeah, until they get to know me, and then they run the other way.

"Maybe he's just shy," she mumbled as she put a piece of sushi in her mouth.

"Shy? With those strange tattoos and piercings all over his body? Unlikely."

"Hey. Don't judge," she said. "Anyway, let's forget about him. Are you sure you want to take me to the airport? It's an early morning flight, and I'd rather take a cab."

"I'm taking you to the airport. No more discussion."

She grinned looking at his scowl. "All righty."

They spoke about work as they finished their meal, and when she was about to leave, she turned and smiled at the tattooed guy who was still staring at her.

He didn't smile back. Instead, he simply continued to stare impassively.

*****

It was almost seven by the time Anika got home from work. Dropping her car keys in a bin next to the main door of her apartment, she headed towards her bedroom. Soon, in what felt like barely seconds later, she was face down on her bed, sprawled on her bed sheets with her hospital scrubs on. She was about to reach the light switch when she saw the light indicating phone messages on her landline, blinking continuously.

Groaning, she got up. Then moving the packed suitcases away from her wardrobe, she grabbed a pair of nightclothes while dialing a number on her cell phone. She sat on her bed, hearing the phone ring.

"Anika! Where were you? I've been trying to reach you all day!"

"Hi, Mom. I was at the hospital, going on rounds and finishing up a lot of things that I needed to do before I leave tomorrow morning."

There was an exasperated sigh. "I know, but seriously, can you not think about this again? Or at least wait until Dad and I get back from our cruise."

"It's okay, Mom. I'll be back before Myra gets home for the holidays."

"Fine," her mom said grudgingly. "But call me often, or at least send me messages. I can check them when I'm at the ports."

"I will, Mom."

They spoke for a few more minutes before her stepfather took the phone from her mom.

"You should take one of those guided tours. They are safe, and you'll get to see a lot in less time."

"Yeah. I have enough vacation accrued, but I can't, Dad. I need to be back in two months."

"All right, kiddo. Have a great journey and do call us if you need anything."

"Yup. And you guys enjoy the rest of your vacation. Love you." Anika ended the call and sighed.

She still felt bone tired due to the back-to-back shifts she had been pulling during the last two weeks.

She got up from the bed and headed towards the bathroom. Stepping into her small yet functional shower, she turned the taps on, and sighed as the warm water began to ease her tensed muscles.

Her mother's words from last week kept repeating in her head. *"Why do you want to go? They never even cared for both of us after your father passed away in an accident."*

It was the day after she received an unexpected call. *"Your grandfather is dying. His last wish is to meet you in person. Please...don't disappoint him."*

Her aunt, who was Anika's father's sister, had called and pleaded with her.

Normally, she wouldn't have dropped everything to rush and see her estranged relatives she had never met, but lately, she had been in a rut. She felt a keen restlessness inside her even though everything was going well with her career and life in general.

Even though her stepfather treated her as one of his own, and she loved her half-sister, Myra, to pieces, she still felt some kind of strange emptiness when it came to having a sense of belonging. That same emptiness even made her think of doing crazy things like maybe agreeing to marry Nathan to start a family of her own, and feel that sense of belonging.

It was the same void that drove her to make plans to visit her family in India. She felt that meeting her relatives and finding out more about her roots would help her find some peace within, and get on with her life as usual.

"All right India. Here I come," she said softly.

CHAPTER THREE

Anika had spent nearly a day on the plane, without much sleep. Surprisingly, she was not tired. She was rather thrilled and excited to be in India.

She wanted to know more about the place where her father grew up and also wanted to see the house he spoke about all the time. As a little girl, she had loved to hear her father's childhood adventures at his ancestral home.

Gathering the last of her three large suitcases from the baggage claim, she headed towards the exit. She scanned the crowd that stood waiting for the arriving passengers, wondering who was going to meet her. Her aunt had told her that the person receiving her at the airport would recognize her.

She had no clue who that would be, since she didn't know anyone in India. She scanned the crowd in a futile effort before pushing her luggage cart to the side.

Just as she was about to reach for her phone to call her aunt, she caught a movement at the corner of her eye. She turned and saw a woman close to her age, approaching her. The woman was dressed in simple, comfortable-looking cotton trousers. She had long thick beautifully plaited hair that contrasted with the brisk manly strides she took.

Anika smiled as she looked into a pair of familiar-looking eyes. It had to be one of her relatives, considering they both had the same light brown eyes.

"Anika?" The woman's voice was brisk, definitely not a tone meant for a friend, let alone a long lost relative.

"Yes," Anika answered with a smile, determined to make an effort to thaw the cold vibes.

The woman did not return her smile. "Let's go."

The woman signaled to the two large burly men who stood behind her like bodyguards. One of the men stepped forward and silently took the luggage cart.

"Oh, that won't be necessary—" Anika's words fell on deaf ears as the man carried her heavy bags quite easily. Clutching her travel purse, she followed the woman who was yet to introduce herself.

She broke into a run to keep up with them as they strode towards the exit. They stopped near an SUV parked right outside the door. It was clearly marked as a no parking zone, but none of the airport security seemed to object. Two more burly men came forward and took the suitcases to another SUV parked behind. The doors of the SUV were held open by the men for Anika and the woman to get in.

"Thank you—" Before Anika could complete, the burly muscled man on her side, shut the door, and slid into the driver's seat.

The woman next to her sat still, without uttering a word while the SUV drove away from the airport

Unable to bear the eerie silence, Anika cleared her throat. "I'm sorry, I didn't get a chance to introduce myself properly. I'm Anika Patel. And you are... ?"

The woman turned towards her with a clenched jaw. Anika was almost sure she wouldn't get a reply, but the woman surprised her by answering.

"Sabitha."

"Nice to meet you, Sabitha. How are we related?"

Sabitha looked at her with mild surprise as though Anika was supposed to know about her already. "Cousins. Our fathers were brothers." Sabitha had a slight accent, and her voice held no emotion as she spoke about their fathers.

Sabitha had said *were* brothers, meaning, Sabitha had lost her father, too. Maybe in the same accident as her father did.

Anika took a moment to suppress the sadness of their loss. "I'm glad to meet you, Sabitha. Hope we become friends while I'm here," she said softly, meaning every word.

She only got a cool nod, making her wonder if she had inadvertently done something to offend her cousin. But another voice inside her head kept questioning why Sabitha wasn't thrilled to see her when their aunt obviously made it seem like her presence was badly needed and wanted.

"How old were you when the... accident happened?"

"Five," came in a curt reply.

Anika wondered if Sabitha ever had a conversation that was more than a monosyllabic response.

"I was almost six when my mom told me that I would never get to see my dad again." Anika's eyes welled up with unexpected tears. Embarrassed, she looked out the window.

There was another stretch of silence. Anika then decided it was best to remain silent until they reached home.

With the SUV powering smoothly through the roads, Anika's eyes drooped as sleep threatened to overtake her. But she didn't want to fall asleep until she had met her father's family. *Her family.*

She continued looking out the window as doubts overtook her again about the impromptu trip. The restlessness that had been hounding her for a while was still there. Then she reminded herself that the place she was going to was a part of her life...her roots.

They spent over an hour in silence before she attempted to start a conversation again. "How much longer to get home?"

"One hour."

"Thanks for coming to the airport this early in the morning. You didn't have to. I could have taken a taxi to the house."

"Neela wanted me to." Sabitha had a strange tone when she said that.

"How is our grandfather doing?"

"Better."

"That's quite good. I'm really looking forward to meet Aunt Neela and our grandfather."

Sabitha turned and looked at her for a couple of seconds with an odd look. "You won't see them until later today. Catch some sleep before you meet them."

"Oh, I'm not too tired to meet them right away—"

"Neela said she would see you in the afternoon." Sabitha said like it was an order from her aunt.

"Oh. Okay." Anika started to feel tired. Maybe it was a good thing that she'd meet everyone after she was well rested.

Settling into the comfortable leather seat, Anika let sleep overcome her. Just as her eyes drooped, she stared at the large tattoo on the driver's neck. Even in her dazed state, the tattoo looked familiar. Before she could analyze further, her brain began to check out.

Her weeklong double shifts were beginning to catch up with her.

***

She woke up to the pleasant sounds of birds chirping. She sat up and stared groggily outside.

The SUV had stopped, and she could see the men unloading her luggage. It was still almost dark, and she could only see the vague details of a large majestic house. Before she could look around and take in her surroundings, Sabita's firm voice interrupted her.

"Follow me."

They passed through two large white marble columns that rose up to the three-story house. The men pushed open a heavily carved, tall wooden door at the main entrance, and took her luggage inside.

She could not register much on the inside. Her cousin strode across a huge open living room, and climbed a flight of stairs, and then walked along a hallway, until she stopped outside a door.

The men followed behind with the luggage, and placed her bags neatly against a wall.

"You'll be staying here until—" Sabitha stop abruptly and cleared her throat. "Until you choose to remain here," she finished.

Anika nodded taking in the surreal surroundings.

"Anything else you need before I leave?" Sabitha asked.

"No."

"I'll get going then. Someone will be here to inform you, and prepare you to meet with our grandfather and Neela."

Anika nodded. "Thank you."

Sabitha and the men left, closing the doors quietly behind them.

Even though she wanted to explore her surroundings right away, she decided to catch a quick nap, and freshen up before her meeting with her family.

CHAPTER FOUR

Anika woke up to an insistent knocking.

"Come in." Her voice was groggy.

A young girl peeked in and slowly walked inside with a shy look.

"Hello." Anika smiled at the girl.

"They asked me to help you get ready, madam. Neelamma will start to receive people in an hour."

Anika found that odd.

"I don't need help in getting ready. I'll be out in thirty minutes." Although her mom and stepdad were doctors, and she and Myra grew up with nannies and maids, they weren't accustomed to people offering to help them get ready for a simple meeting with family.

The girl stood uncertainly for a few seconds before she nodded and left.

Anika stepped down from the bed, slowly looking around the room. She had been too tired to notice the details before, but now she observed everything. She had slept on a traditional four-poster bed in a large room with high ceilings. The walls gleamed with the antique oil paintings with various subtle pastel colors.

The antique clock against the wall indicated it was eleven fifteen. Sabitha and the girl whose name she had forgotten to ask had told that her aunt received her guests at noon. She found the appointment system to be odd within the family members, but didn't want to read too much into it.

Pulling her stuff out of the suitcases, she quickly got ready. She gave herself one final glance in the mirror before stepping out of the room.

She had chosen to wear traditional clothes out of respect to her grandfather, even though she wasn't entirely comfortable with the slightly revealing clothes. Growing up in the West, she was used to wearing leg-baring or even shoulder-baring clothes. But the traditional clothes, although modest when it came to shoulders and legs, usually showed a good amount of bare midriff. Maybe the next day, she could wear her usual. She was quite relieved to see Sabitha in cotton trousers and a blouse that morning, indicating that people weren't very conservative with the dressing.

She walked towards a window and took in a breath of fresh air to calm her nerves. The hint of greenery she had seen on her way from the airport was replaced with an endless brown landscape.

Outside the window, she could hear the noises of bustling activity. There were vague hums of excited conversations. Curious and oddly nervous at the same time, she took another deep breath, and walked out from her room.

The first thing she saw was the indoor balcony which ran along the inside of the house, overlooking the center area. She walked to the railing and looked down to the ground level, to see if anyone was gathered inside the impressive-looking living area.

It was mostly empty with only a couple of maids cleaning the various antique pieces adorning the room. To one side, she saw a large dining room where Sabitha was speaking to an elderly man in a wheelchair.

That must be Grandfather.

Anika hurried down the stairs, her shoes making enough noise to indicate her arrival. Sabitha looked up and nodded to her in acknowledgement with a dispassionate look.

Taking a deep breath, Anika ignored the growing discomfort that threatened to envelop her, and kept her eyes trained on the elderly man in the wheelchair.

"Hello, Grandfather," she greeted quietly, feeling her heart tug at the gaunt and shriveled face of her father's dad.

The man in front of her must have suffered greatly, having lost both his sons and his wife in an accident. She could even understand to some extent, why he had shunned his son's wife and daughter during his grief. Her aunt had mentioned that he had lost his voice after his paralysis attack many years ago.

At the moment, he was watching her with a confused look on his face.

"That's Anika," Sabitha explained to him softly. "Uncle Yashwant's daughter."

Sabitha's words made her grandfather's eyes come alive.

Anika couldn't make out whether it was with happiness or anger. Her mother had told her a few years ago that Anika's father's family was not happy about their eldest son marrying a girl they had not chosen or approved. It was one of the main reasons why they did not want Anika or her mother to visit them after his accidental death.

"I'm here to see you, Grandfather. I hope you are doing well."

Her grandfather grunted in response.

A few minutes of awkward silence ensued. It was shattered by the sound of a heavy door creaking open.

"Send her in!" A familiar voice of a woman boomed from above, resounding loudly within the living room.

CHAPTER FIVE

Anika felt something build up in her stomach, making her feel a little queasy about the entire situation. She turned to look at Sabitha, but her cousin, as usual, was expressionless.

"Come." Sabitha went up the stairs, but walked in the opposite direction of the room that had been offered to Anika that morning.

As soon as they reached one of the doorways, Sabitha stopped short.

"Go. She's waiting for you." Sabitha indicated to a partially open door.

"Aunt Neelambari?" The queasiness continued..

"Yes."

"Aren't you coming inside?" Anika asked Sabitha when she saw her cousin turn away.

Sabitha stopped and turned back. "No."

"Sabitha, please. Can you stay for a few minutes—"

"I'm not allowed inside. You'll have to go in by yourself." Anika saw her cousin's eyes flare. For the first time, there was some emotion on her cousin's face.

Rage? Sorrow? Anika didn't know. She was too worried about herself to analyze her cousin's reaction.

Her rational mind began to reason. *Come on, Anika. It's just your aunt. You spoke to her on the phone and liked her.*

Her aunt had convinced her to travel to India to meet her terminally sick grandfather. But her grandfather didn't appear to be ill, at least not in the way she had imagined him to be. She had expected a bedridden man with whom she would have a tearful reunion with.

Taking a deep breath, she gathered her courage and walked into a dimly-lit room.

As her eyes adjusted, she noticed it was a large suite with multiple rooms. The doors of the other rooms were firmly shut.

"So, you are finally here."

Anika jumped when she heard her aunt speak.

"Aunt Neelambari?" Anika couldn't find her immediately within the almost dark room.

"Yes," an impatient reply came. "Come here. Come closer to me."

Anika blinked several times until her eyes adjusted to the dim lighting. She saw the outline of a woman seated in what appeared to be a rocking chair with her feet propped up. Slowly, she went towards the woman, and stopped next to her.

"Kneel down." The order was thrown sternly, raising her hackles. Anika decided to ignore her reaction, attributing it to her aunt being eccentric, rather than rude.

As soon as she knelt down, she felt her aunt grab her face. She also felt her aunt's eyes peering at her, making her feel extremely uncomfortable.

"Jaya!"

"Yes, madam," a meek reply from a woman came from somewhere.

"Open the curtains!" There was excitement in her aunt's voice.

There was a shuffling of footsteps, and then the noise of curtains being opened sounded in the room, followed by a blinding light.

Anika flinched as the bright light hit her eyes, which had just adjusted to the dim lighting. She tried to move her head, but she was still held within her aunt's firm grip.

Slowly she opened her eyes, only to see a shockingly similar image of herself.

Her aunt looked just like her.

Or rather she looked just like her aunt. The resemblance was eerily uncanny.

Her aunt had a pale face which still looked quite youthful. She also had liberal streaks of gray in her hair, making her appear regal. She wore a heavy, ornate sari that had weaves of gold and magenta in it.

Neelambari let out a booming laugh. "By God, this is happening now for sure!"

Confused, Anika simply stared at her for an explanation.

"Jaya! Open the balcony doors. Tell the people to gather outside right now!"

"Yes, madam!" The maid opened the balcony doors where noise from a crowd was heard.

Jaya hurried outside the room. Anika could hear noises from several footsteps going down the stairs.

"What is happening?" Anika asked her aunt. "I thought Grandfather called for me because he was on his deathbed. I-I just met him. He seemed fine."

Her aunt ignored her words. She didn't let go of Anika's face. Her eyes roved over each and every feature with a satisfying smile that bordered on maniacal.

The crowd outside became deafening.

Anika wondered what was happening even as some instinct warned her to pull her face away and run out of the place.

Her aunt's hands slid down over her arms. Gripping them tightly, she stood and pulled Anika up with her. "Come. They are waiting for you."

"Who?"

Ignoring Anika's question, her aunt pulled her towards the open doors leading to a balcony, until they stood staring down at a large crowd.

"Thirty years!" Her aunt's voice boomed even louder. "Thirty years of my penance is about to pay off. I stand in front of you today, because we finally have a way to break the curse!"

Her aunt's voice was commanding. The crowd fell silent as they listened to her in rapt attention. "Anika Prajapati will soon become Anika Singham and continue the Singham bloodlines!"

As soon as her aunt finished saying those cryptic words, there was a deafening roar from the cheering crowd.

CHAPTER SIX

"What is Singham? What are you talking about?" Anika's heart thudded loudly as her uneasiness began to turn into a full-blown panic. Her aunt ignored her questions as she was still turned towards the crowd, addressing them.

"I'm ending my penance today to step out of the house for the first time in thirty years. And my first place to visit will be...the Singham temple."

There were loud murmurs. Anika saw her cousin, Sabitha, among the crowd. Sabitha was watching her with another mysteriously blank look.

Her aunt turned away from the crowd to finally look at Anika. "Come."

Anika followed behind her aunt, not because of the regal order, but to know what was happening, and why she was being involved in something that had to do with so many people.

Her aunt walked towards the door, and stopped short of the doorstep, with one foot raised above the floor. Then taking a deep breath, she stepped outside the room.

Anika walked behind her, until they stood in front of the wheelchair where her grandfather was watching his daughter with tears in his eyes.

Neelambari bent down to touch his feet. "I have broken my penance, Papa. I will now restore our family line. There will soon be a Singham heir in the Prajapati household."

She turned towards Anika. "And your granddaughter will make it happen."

Anika had heard enough. "Tell me what is happening. Who are all those people? And what is Singham?"

"Not what? Who?" Her aunt replied and walked over to one of the ornate sofas and sat down with her arms raised on top of the high armrests. She was watching Anika with immense satisfaction.

"The Singhams have been—and *are* still—the most powerful, influential, and prosperous family in this province. "

"Okay. But what have *I* got to do with them or any of it?" Anika asked, getting impatient due to her gut feeling that was ringing several warning bells inside her.

Her aunt's smile grew. "Everything, my love. The current Singham heir, Abhay Singham will make you his wife in two days."

"What?" Anika was sure it was some sort of a local joke she didn't understand or get.

"You heard me. The fearless and ferocious Abhay Singham will soon be your husband. Your life is honored that he agreed to have you bear his heir and continue the Singham bloodlines."

"What are you even talking about?" Anika frowned as anxiety began to take over.

"This land has been cursed with a drought for the past thirty years. People are dying every day, and the only way to break the curse—is if a woman from Prajapati or Senani families bore an heir to the Singhams."

It had to be a nightmare. Who talks about curses in this day and age?

Anika took a deep breath to calm her nerves and also her need to burst out with a rude response. "I appreciate that you think I can somehow help with the drought, but I'm only here because you said grandfather is sick. Unfortunately, I might have to cut short my trip—"

Her aunt laughed. "How polite you are, my love. I was expecting fireworks and explosion. It's also very sweet of you to think we are going to offer you with a choice."

Anika felt her body stiffen as she listened to the underlying veiled threat. "I don't appreciate being threatened. I'm leaving right now. You don't have to drop me off anywhere. I'll call a taxi."

She had taken a few steps before she stopped short due to her aunt's next words.

"If you are going up to look for your phone, you won't find it. You won't have access to the rest of the world unless I allow you to."

Anika's legs trembled at the threat, but she stood tall and swung back to face her aunt. "I'm twenty-six-years-old. You cannot stop me if I want to leave. No one can."

Her aunt smiled. "Ah. She does have some backbone." She turned to look at Sabitha who had joined them and was quietly listening. "See, I told you, Sabi. You said you wanted to be the queen because your cousin doesn't have the guts or backbone to rule next to Abhay Singham. Look at her now. She will definitely be able to tame the ferocious beast." There was a proud look on Neelambari's face.

Sabitha didn't respond.

Anika shook her head. "I don't care what you all think of me. This was a mistake and I'm leaving right now." She began walking towards the stairway.

"Myra is pretty sweet. Pity her life is going to be cut short at the age of twenty."

Anika froze.

"Just because I haven't stepped out of my room in thirty years, it doesn't mean I'm stupid or powerless." Her aunt spoke in a quiet tone that raised goosebumps on her skin. "If you care about the safety of your mother, her husband, and your half-sister, you will do as I say."

Anika turned to look at her aunt. "You're lying. You can't harm them. I'll warn them. They are safe—"

"Safe for now. But for how long...it all depends on you."

Anika shook off the threats and turned to leave. This time she headed towards the main door. She had to get out of this house first. She'd come back for her stuff later or send someone to get it from there.

"She doesn't believe us, Sabi. Tell her what little Myra is doing right now." Her aunt's tone was playful.

"Myra is with her friends at a party held on her university campus."

"And Mr. and Mrs. Patel?"

"Their cruise ship is docked in Spain," Sabitha answered in a robotic voice, but it was enough to make Anika freeze on the spot.

"Ah, she believes us now, Sabi. Maybe if she doesn't, we should probably bring Myra here to keep her company."

Anika swung towards them. "If you harm my little sister in any way, I will—"

Before she could complete her threat, her aunt cut her off. "Keep quiet! This is the first and last time you will take that tone with me. I didn't spend thirty years of my life in solitude for nothing."

Anika stood still, various thoughts and emotions running inside her head trying to come up with a logical explanation.

"What if I don't want anything to do with this?" Anika asked in a calm tone.

"Oh, you will. And willingly too."

"I will tell that man...Abhay Singham that I'm being forced to do this. He'll refuse to marry me then—" She broke off to her aunt's loud laugh.

Her aunt threw back her head while laughing, and then she shook her head in amusement. "My dear niece. Abhay Singham is a *beast*. He can kill a person with his bare hands, without batting an eyelid. He will do anything for the people living in this province. And the people want... you."

Fear locked Anika's throat at her aunt's words and the description of the man.

"Three more hours...and you'll meet your future husband at the Singham temple."

CHAPTER SEVEN

Anika sat on the bed with her arms wrapped around her raised knees. Almost an hour had passed since the revelations. Everything felt surreal, and she badly wanted to wake up from the nightmare.

Anika's phone had gone missing, and there were no landlines or computers available. She was completely cut off from her world to be left at her aunt's mercy.

I can't just sit here and do nothing. I need to get help and not drown in self-pity!

The knock on the door interrupted her thoughts, but Anika didn't respond. She knew it wasn't her aunt or Sabitha because they wouldn't bother knocking.

"Madam, I brought your lunch." A soft voice of a woman came through the door.

Maybe the maid can help.

"Come in!"

The maid wheeled in a cart with silver dishes placed on top. The aroma emitting from the food made Anika's stomach even queasier. She was too nervous to think of eating right then.

"Do you need anything else, madam?" the maid asked with a polite smile.

"Yes. A phone."

The maid's eyes fell. "I'm sorry, madam. We were instructed not to allow you to speak with anyone outside this house, or even help you leave."

Anika wanted to lash out, but she knew the maid was only following orders.

She didn't know whom to ask for help. She only knew Sabitha. Even though Sabitha appeared cold and unfeeling, the fact that they were cousins by blood should somehow compel the other woman to help.

"Where is Sabitha? I want to speak with her."

The maid looked scared and didn't answer.

"You said, I'm not allowed to speak with anyone outside the house. Sabitha lives here. So tell me where she is."

The maid bit her lip uncertainly. "Sabitha madam is...busy."

"Where is she? I'll go find her."

"She's downstairs in the—" The maid broke off, paling rapidly. "I-I don't know where she is."

Anika didn't believe her, but she didn't want to push the maid too much. "Thanks. That's it for now. Maybe I'll speak with her later when she comes to me."

The maid nodded and left hurriedly with the door clicking shut behind her. As soon as the receding footsteps of the maid could barely be heard, Anika got down from the bed, and moved towards the bedroom door.

She turned the knob and luckily it was not locked. Her aunt must have been incredibly confident that she wouldn't try to escape.

Slowly, she opened the door, and looked outside into the empty hallway. She crept through the hall, her bare feet hardly making any sound. And instead of going down the main stairs that led to the large living room, she continued until she saw another flight of stairs that seemed to lead to a lower level.

She continued down the stairs until she reached the floor that seemed to be at the basement level. The hallway was dimly lit. As she moved along, she could hear the faint sounds of a man gasping, and water being splashed.

Was that a bathroom? She wasn't sure because she heard voices of other men and also a woman's that sounded much like that of her cousin's.

Her heart began to beat loudly as she walked closer, and then stopped in front of a door, where she could hear the voices even more clearly. Taking a deep breath, she slowly opened the door a few inches.

There were four men, along with Sabitha, standing with their backs facing the door. They were watching something. No, not something. Someone. That someone was gasping and coughing.

"More." As soon as Sabitha passed the order, one of the burly men moved and picked up a large bucket. As soon as the burly man moved, Anika saw another man, tied to a chair.

Water was poured on his head, more or less drowning him. Soon there was more gasping, followed by sobbing. "P-please! Stop!"

"Then give me the name," Sabitha demanded softly.

"K-Karunakar Reddy. Please, stop. No more! No more!" The man sobbed and begged.

Sabitha raised her hand, indicating to the man holding another bucket of water to stop.

"P-please, forgive me. Give me a last chance!" The man's sobs grew louder, even though the torture with the water had stopped.

"You know I never give another chance to anyone. You make a mistake, you die," Sabitha stated calmly.

One of the men handed something to Sabitha. Only when it gleamed in the faint light, did Anika realize that it was a gun. A scream got lodged into her throat with fear.

"Please!" The man began to beg. "I have a family. My wife is pregnant. J-just give me another c-chance."

Sabitha sighed audibly, and then she fired not once, not twice, but repeatedly, only stopping when the lifeless body of the man slumped in the chair.

She handed back the gun to one of the men. "Clear up this mess and get ready. We have to leave to the temple in an hour."

The men nodded at Sabitha's instruction. Two men began untying the dead man, and started rolling his body in plastic, while two other men began to clear the blood on the ground.

The scream lodged in Anika's throat was finally let loose. She screamed out shrilly and shook violently. She vomited on the floor next to her, but since she hadn't eaten anything all day, they were only dry heaves.

She trembled as footsteps drew closer to her. When she raised her bleary eyes, she saw the bloody shirt and trousers of her cousin.

"Y-you killed him! You killed a man! How could you? How—" Sabitha grabbed Anika's arms, pulled her up and shook her until her hysteria died. Only her sobs remained.

"How did you know I was here?" Sabitha demanded.

"You killed a man. You deliberately took a life of a person," Anika whispered as tears continued pouring out of her eyes.

Her cousin's eyes hardened. "Not my first time and it won't be the last either. So shut up and get back to your room. Come down when you are called. Go!"

With her body still trembling in shock, Anika ran towards the stairway. She couldn't recall how she found her room, but as soon as she got in, she shut it and locked it from the inside.

The scene she had witnessed began to play again and again behind her eyes, especially the part where the man was begging for his life, and also pleading because his wife was pregnant.

Her cousin was a heartless monster! She killed the man in cold blood.

Anika cried at the helplessness she felt, being trapped in the hellhole with absolutely no one to help escape.

*****

Anika didn't know how long she lay curled on the bed in a fetal position, but she jerked when she heard insistent knocking on the door.

"Madam, everyone is waiting for you. They have asked me to help you get ready."

Rubbing her eyes with the back of her hand, she curled up even tighter.

"Madam, I-I was told that if I didn't return with you in thirty minutes, I will be punished. P-please...open the door." The woman's voice on the other side of the door trembled.

Anika's heart began to thud loudly. *Was there no low my aunt and cousin would stoop to? How could they threaten a person for someone else's actions?*

Reluctantly, she dragged herself from the bed and opened the door. The same maid who had come that morning, stood with an uncertain look, holding a large bag.

"I-I brought clothes and other accessories for you to get ready."

Anika nodded jerkily and moved away from the door. She didn't want to change or get ready to meet a man she had no interest in seeing, let alone marry. She wanted to shout out those words, but she didn't want to get the maid in trouble or even get killed because of her.

She went to the large bathroom within her room and splashed some cold water on her tear-swollen face. She came out and let the maid help her get ready.

The heavy ornate lehenga and a cropped blouse with endless buttons at the back did require the maid's help.

Anika objected to the styling of her hair, and also to wearing the jewelry that was sent up. However, each time she objected, the maid's eyes lit up in fear, and she had to just let the maid complete the task given to her.

"All done, madam. You look very beautiful. The Singhams will be more than impressed."

Anika nodded, not bothering to look at herself in the mirror.

"We have five more minutes. Sabitha and madam are very particular about time. Please hurry!"

Slipping into comfortable shoes which didn't match her ornate outfit, but were covered by the long lehenga, Anika followed behind the maid.

Sabitha was already waiting downstairs, dressed in a similar outfit. Anika was shocked at her cousin's transformation. The woman in front of her barely looked like the heartless monster that had killed a man in cold blood.

Sabitha's eyes scanned her quickly, probably making sure she had followed the orders. "Let's go. Neela is already in the car. She doesn't like to be kept waiting."

Anika quietly followed behind her cousin. Right outside the main door, there were two SUVs parked, packed with men. In the middle was a luxury car, where her aunt was waiting impatiently at the back seat.

"Let's go. I don't want the Singhams to think that Prajapati women are tardy."

The door was held open, but Anika hesitated.

Neelambari held a large silver tray with things one carried when they visited temples.

Instead of snapping at Anika to hurry, Neelambari smiled widely with an approving look. "You look radiant, my dear. You will knock that Singham warrior off his feet."

"Come." Neelambari patted to the empty seat next to her. "Sit next to me."

Neelambari spoke in a sweet tone. The same tone she had used when she had called Anika a few weeks ago. But instead of affection, all Anika felt for her aunt was fear and disgust.

Not having a choice, Anika slid next to Neelambari and sat stiffly.

Sabitha sat in the front, next to the driver, even though there was enough room in the backseat.

"To the Singham temple." Neelambari's voice hummed with excitement.

CHAPTER EIGHT

The ride to the Singham temple was mostly quiet. Apart from *"A lot has changed in the last thirty years,"* comment from her aunt, there was no other talk.

An hour or so later, after staring blindly at the scenery outside, Anika noticed that the car was slowing down. There were dozens of people fleeing something.

"What's happening?" Neelambari asked. "Sabitha, go check."

Sabitha stiffened at the order, but she got out of the car. Anika could see a gun in Sabitha's hands that she was trying to conceal behind her. But considering Sabitha had worn ethnic wear with no pockets, it was impossible to carry a concealed weapon. Soon, Sabitha disappeared behind the crowd.

When most of the people had fled, Anika could see dozens of people fighting right outside the temple entrance.

The sight in front of her was brutal. Anika's eyes fell on a tall man whose features she could not see from the car. He was pounding someone. The other man fell, but the beating continued until a splatter of blood fell on the tall man's face. He then moved on to the next man who came at him. The tall man grabbed the other man's head and banged it against a boulder, until the blood ran over the stone.

Anika gasped out loud watching the brutal scene.

"What is it?" She heard her aunt ask, but the bile threatening to shoot up didn't allow her to answer.

"What did you see—" Her aunt's voice abruptly broke off as she stared at the sight in front of her. "Vijay..." That name came out of her aunt's lips like a prayer. The rapt, proud and satisfied look on her aunt's face made Anika even sicker.

The large man was now tackling yet another person. He grabbed that person by the neck and beat his face repeatedly to the side of a car, until that person had either died or fainted.

"Vijay Singham..."

Slowly, Neelambari blinked as though she was coming out of a trance. "No. Not Vijay. That must be his son... Abhay Singham. Your soon-to-be husband."

Anika was sure she was going to throw up.

One of the men who had driven her from the airport, ran towards their car, and got in the front seat where Sabitha had been sitting. He was bleeding profusely.

"Madam, we are under attack from the Senanis. They found out we would be meeting the Singhams here. We have been asked by Abhay Singham to leave. He has informed us that he will come to the Prajapati house tomorrow for the wedding preparations."

Small pinging noises sounded as something hit their car and the windows.

"We are being shot at! We have to leave right now, madam." "Let's go!" Neelambari instructed.

The car began to drive away.

"What about Sabitha?" Anika asked in a panic. Even though her cousin turned out to be a cold-blooded murderer, Anika cared for her in the basic human sense. Being a doctor, she only knew how to save lives, not take them away in senseless violence.

"Sabitha will have to get back in the other cars," her aunt casually stated as though she gave a damn about her other niece.

"But people have guns. She must need our help—"

Her aunt turned towards her, watching in amusement, even as Anika's panic grew. "Don't worry. Your cousin is not that helpless. She's going to live." The smile turned into mild admiration. "If that girl weren't born a mongrel, she would have been the right fit to carry the Singham bloodlines. Unfortunately her father, my youngest brother, chose to slum. Not that your father did any good, but the only saving grace was that your mother was at least a high-born, even if her family line is not in the least impressive."

Anika didn't understand half of the things her aunt was saying to her. The only thing on her mind was to focus and plan on getting away from the hell she was dragged into.

CHAPTER NINE

The tall figure approached her slowly, not caring for the guns firing in the background. The air was muggy from the bloodshed, and so dusty that she couldn't see the man's face.

She couldn't see her aunt or Sabitha either, and her first thought was to run.

She gathered her energy, preparing to escape, but she was stuck inside a car that was locked from the outside.

The man was getting closer. She could see his crisp white long shirt smeared with blood. She knew it was the blood of the people he must have brutally killed with no conscience.

She didn't want to be anywhere close to him. She had to escape now!

She moved her legs but they seemed paralyzed.

She was stuck as the monster drew even closer.

Anika woke up with a gasp.

She was lying on a bed, sweating and shaking. Her heart was pounding in her chest, threatening to burst out. She shook her head, hoping to wipe out the nightmare that still left fear and anxiety in her mind. It wasn't just a nightmare, it was real—her reality.

Still trembling, she slowly sat up on the bed, noticing she was all alone in the same room she had been in the previous morning.

Had it only been twenty-four hours since she got here? It felt like an eternity. She had seen and experienced so much within a day—it threatened to drive her into a state of shock. She didn't react to the clock ticking somewhere in the room, taking her closer to D-day.

It was the day before her reckoning.

In one more day, she was to be offered as a sacrificial lamb to a man who was more of a beast. And she had no choice or say in it.

She was now resigned to the fact that she was trapped inside a fortress, both physically and mentally, with no escape. Even if she could somehow find a way out of the house, it would be at the cost of her family.

Tears gathered in her eyes as she recalled her loved ones. She missed them. She wanted to hug them, until she knew they were going to be safe and free from any threats.

Stifling the urge to break into hysterical sobs, she got out of bed and walked towards the large window. The outside was bustling with activity. People scrambled around, filling the courtyard with flowers and other decorations.

The entire area was being decorated as far as the eye could see. The long road leading to the house from the main street was lined with banana tree trunks, connected by endless rows of flowers. The harsh concrete walls that were surely splashed with blood at some point, gleamed with new life making her feel even deader on the inside.

Like everyone her age, she had thought about her wedding day before, but never in a million years did she imagine it to be the way it was—out of her control. It wasn't just her marriage, she had no control over her life, and that infuriated her. She was being reduced to a pawn on the chessboard that was being manipulated and sacrificed for the sake of the ruthless players.

How can I simply resign myself?

What else can you do?

With that defeated reply, it felt like she was not the same person she had been before. Most of her life, she had thrived on challenges and overcoming obstacles, but right then, she couldn't come up with a way to get out of the mess.

She walked away from the window, and opened the door that led to a small balcony overlooking the back of the house. She took in the wide expanse of the barren brown land. Her fingers gripped the balcony rails as she recalled that the people believed the drought was due to a curse and not the effect of a climate change.

"That won't kill you." Neelambari's voice cut through her haze.

Anika didn't turn around, and kept her eyes focused on a faraway spot.

"If you were considering ending your life by jumping off the balcony, you'll only break a leg, and look horrible in your wedding pictures."

Anika refused to react to the taunt because she knew she had no fight left in her—not at that moment.

"Prajapati women have the blood of the royals in them. They would never consider self-harm. But if you were indeed considering it, then it's probably evident that your mom must have strayed."

Anika's blood boiled at the slur on her mother. She swung towards the woman who was her father's sister. "Stop it!" she hissed.

"Oh... I'm sorry if I hurt you. I shouldn't have said that about your mother. I don't know what happens to me sometimes."

The sudden shift in her aunt's tone scared Anika more than anything. Her aunt was like a chameleon, changing her behavior at will, never really showing her true colors.

Striding over to the small patio sofa, her aunt patted the seat next to her. "Come, please sit here."

Anika ignored the request.

Her aunt sighed as though she was dealing with a stubborn child. "This may all seem bad to you, Anika, but soon you'll realize you are only embracing your destiny and helping with the greater good."

"Don't. I don't want to listen to any of that again." She still couldn't wrap that insane reason—of curses and droughts leading to her marriage—around her head.

Her aunt gave her a shrewd look. "Well, I will leave you to enjoy your solitude. But remember, no trying to escape or think that you have a way out of this marriage. You will get married tomorrow, or you will regret it for the rest of your life."

"I already regret everything that has to do with coming here."

"Not as much as you would, if you try to oppose any of the plans I've made. One phone call to the men watching your sister and parents, and you'll not have a family living in the U.S. anymore." Her aunt's voice held a raw menace.

Anika clenched her fists in anger, not saying anything.

There was a chilling smile. "You know, maybe all this reluctance is also because your heart might have been otherwise occupied by a different man." Neelambari tapped a finger on her cheek as though lost in thought. "Nathan... is it? One of my men informed me of a white boy who follows behind you like a love-sick puppy."

Anika then realized why the tattoo on the man's neck who picked her up from the airport, looked familiar. She had seen it from a distance on the man Nathan had warned her about. The man who had been following them in San Francisco.

"Don't hurt him," Anika whispered as fear and worry took over. "Nathan's innocent in all this. Please. I'll do as you say."

"Oh, that you will, my dear. And even when I'm not saying anything, you will cooperate with me. I not only have men following your family and close friends, but I also have their phones tapped and emails hacked. So if you think all you need is a phone access to get out of this, you are wrong. Dead wrong." Neelambari smiled at the pun. "One wrong word from your mouth, complaining to your husband, or anyone to that matter, about your family being held hostage, it will be equivalent to their death warrant. There is no way out. Even if you die by your own hand or by someone else's, I won't spare any of your loved ones."

Anika sat in shock, listening to the threats.

Neelambari got up with a satisfied smile on her face. "I think you are smart enough to understand what is at stake here. I'll see you tomorrow, then." Just before Neelambari opened the bedroom door to leave, she turned to look at Anika with an affectionate smile.

"Enjoy your last day as Anika Prajapati, my love. Because tomorrow, you'll be Anika Singham."

CHAPTER TEN

Anika stared back at the reflection of a terrified woman in the mirror. With trembling lips and widened eyes, she didn't recognize herself.

Despair welled up within her again as a feeling of extreme hopelessness enveloped her, for not being able to stop what was happening in her life. "She is going to ruin her makeup if she doesn't stop crying," one of the women told someone..

Anika's vision blurred as she continued trembling, but none of the dozen women around her seemed to care for her tears.

"I don't know why she's sad. It's supposed to be the happiest day of her life," one of the women grumbled.

The other women made several noises in agreement and simply went about decking her up like clockwork. They tugged and styled her hair, putting endless jewelry on her. They refused to recognize her state of despair, making her feel like she was an inanimate object with no feelings.

Bile rose in her throat as she tried to sit through their ministrations quietly. She didn't feel the happiness or anticipation she had dreamt of about the occasion.

The occasion being her wedding.

"Look at her. I need to fix her face again," complained a woman, and began dabbing something under her eyes, to get rid of the moisture stains.

Didn't anyone from this godforsaken place have any compassion or basic humanity?

Losing her cool, Anika hissed, and grabbed the thing from the woman's hands, and smashed it against the mirror. The antique mirror which had apparently been in her so-called family for several generations, cracked loudly.

There were several gasps around the room, and then pin-drop silence. The only sounds made were of her rampage.

"Leave me alone!" Anika shouted. "Why don't you all leave me alone!"

She shoved away the boxes of jewelry, makeup, and everything else placed on the dressing table to the floor. A million things hit the marble flooring with a loud crash.

She was a generally a peaceful person who took pride at being rational. But at that very moment, even her rational mind wanted her to smash and destroy everything and anyone in her path.

She was becoming a savage. *They* were turning her into a savage, just like them.

When cornered, one apparently fought with everything they had. She wanted to, very badly, but she couldn't fight back. They had her trapped.

She kept screaming and crying, kicking at the objects that rolled at her feet, and threw the other exclusive things that were brought in for the wedding.

A deep, commanding voice made her stop in her tracks.

"Get out. Everyone." A man's voice jolted her from her outburst.

"Sir. You can't be here," a wavering voice of a woman began to say. "It is considered bad luck—" The woman stopped speaking all of the sudden, and a loaded silence fell in the room.

"Trust me. It'll be even worse if anyone tries to stop me." The man's voice stated in a chilling, dead calm tone that caused goosebumps to break out on her skin.

Anika heard the rustling as everyone began to hurriedly clear the room, and went out of the door. She froze, wondering if she should grab the brief opportunity of freedom, and go along with them, but the cold voice of the man issued another command. "The bride stays."

She remained frozen.

When everyone left, there was absolute silence.

"Turn around and look at me," the man ordered quietly.

Trembling, and worried about the consequences, she slowly turned, raising her eyes towards the man.

Her vision was still blurry from the residual moisture.

She wiped her tears away and was met with the sight of the broad back of a tall man as he closed the door shut. Stepping back, she wrapped her arms around her protectively. She kept her wary eyes trained on him, waiting for what, she didn't know.

As soon as he turned, she felt like the air was sucked away from around the room, making her gasp out loud.

He looked larger than life. And more importantly, he looked like he could easily kill her with a single blow.

But the man who intimidated her badly wasn't looking at her. His eyes first scanned the mess she had made, and then they slowly returned to her face to look at her dispassionately. She expected to see anger, but there was none.

He didn't say anything for a long moment, just kept his eyes firmly locked on her face.

After an indeterminate amount of time, he broke the deafening silence. "So. You are my bride-to-be," he stated, rather than asked, in a deep voice.

The word 'bride' broke through her trance and made adrenaline course through her body.

God, this is so messed up. Why am I cowering in fear?

She knew she cannot—and *should* not—give up her fight because of brute force. She was a problem solver, a logical thinker who had succeeded most of her life convincing people to think from her perspective. She should be able to use reasoning to invoke some compassion within the man whom she was supposed to marry.

"I don't want this," she whispered, unable to work up a louder voice. She kept her eyes on his face, pleading. "Please stop this marriage."

He didn't respond and neither did he react in anyway.

Come on, try more. Keep trying! The voice in her head kept shouting at her.

She gathered her courage to reason with him, but she knew next to nothing about him. Just what she had heard and seen the previous day.

She shuddered, trying hard not to recall the events that still shocked her. The facts would only traumatize her again, and put her in a position where she wouldn't be able to reason anymore.

With great effort, she kept her eyes on the man's face.

Under the large skylight, the man didn't look like a monster the first glance—far from it. He was elegantly dressed and also good looking with perfectly chiseled features. He also appeared to be close to her age.

But when she looked beyond the superficial cover, she noticed the truth. His eyes, although beautifully dark and intense, were also vacant of any emotions. They appeared cold, dead, and soulless. *Like that of a monster who could beat someone to death.*

His clothes were neat and very expensive looking, but she couldn't avoid tearing her eyes away from his bruised and slightly swollen knuckles. She shuddered as she recalled the violence she had witnessed the previous day.

As she stood in front of the disturbing stranger, she realized the odds were stacked heavily against her. It would be next to impossible to convince someone like him of anything.

He would be the kind to throw around orders, not listen to a rational discussion. She knew she had a slim chance, but she had to fight back or even beg her way to freedom.

"I don't want this wedding," she repeated. "We can think of another solution. We should be able to come up with a reasonable... " her voice trailed off when she saw him compressing his lips into a thin hard line as he began to walk towards her.

Her pulse sped up, beating wildly against her throat. Her heart began to pound hard in her chest until it ached. She wanted to scream and run away in fear, but she held her ground, keeping her eyes trained on him.

Through trembling lips, she spoke again. "I'm not from your world. I don't belong in this place. Let me get back to my family," she reasoned.

She was close to being thrown back into a state of shock, reminding her once again that she was living in a nightmare. In a land of no rules, or humanity, or any compassion.

The man stopped in front of her until he was too close for comfort. She had to raise her eyes to look at him. She flinched at the look he was directing towards her.

His eyes were locked on her face as his mouth stretched into a sneer full of hate. "We are getting married *because* your precious family has been begging me to do so. So if you, or your fucking family, tries to pull any stunts during our wedding today, attempting to back out, I'm not going to spare anyone." He spat out the words 'your family' like they were a curse.

Slowly and deliberately, his eyes swept over her body dressed in traditional bridal attire. "Nothing and no one—including you—can stop this from happening. You will become my wife by tonight," he vowed.

Listening to those words, her legs gave out from under, and she collapsed on her knees, unable to swallow the defeat.

How could she have let herself be trapped in this hellhole? Because of her one impulsive decision to meet her estranged family, she was going to lose everything.

Her freedom and also her soul.

CHAPTER ELEVEN

Chanting of prayers filled the air, as several priests performed the wedding ceremony around a large fire pit, on top of a decorated stage. Hundreds of lavishly dressed men and women were assembled around a large courtyard to witness the wedding.

As the ceremony progressed, the guests from the bride and groom's side watched each other warily as they stood tensely. Even through the numbness, Anika felt a palpable tension among the wedding guests.

Except for her aunt, Neelambari.

Anika noticed that her aunt had a satisfied smile that bordered on manic as she watched the wedding take place. Sabitha was conspicuously missing.

Anika's grandfather was seated in a wheelchair next to his daughter, watching everything with a grim look.

"Sir, the wedding is now over. You and your wife are now free to take blessings from your guests," the priest announced in a shaky voice.

During the very few weddings, Anika had attended in her twenty-six years, she had noticed that the groom always smiled proudly after the wedding. He did so, because he felt like he had accomplished something wonderful, and even the bride always smiled back.

But her newly wedded husband smiled grimly and calmly at the tense faces of the Prajapati family. Even through her daze, Anika noticed the smile didn't reach his eyes.

Not that Anika herself had bothered to smile at anyone. On the outside, she looked angry and stubborn. But in truth, she was so frantic that she could barely sit still during the main ceremony as panicked gasps escaped her. She had been praying for a miracle to occur—some last minute, desperate miracle that would free her from these people.

"Come." The man next to her—her husband—held her elbow.

Anika jerked away, her stomach churning with fear and resentment at having to endure his touch. When he had threatened her earlier that day, she was in too much of a shock. Later, she slowly decided she was making things very easy for him and her father's family. They have been getting away with a lot of things, leaving her no choice but to follow them.

The groom frowned, his handsome, cruel face hardened. He held her elbow with a tighter grip and dragged her to another decorated dais where two heavily carved, golden throne-like chairs were placed.

Anika was more or less pushed into one of them and her groom sat on the other. A steady stream of guests came to congratulate and bless them.

"Fuck!"

The crude word brought Anika out of the numbness. She turned to look at the man who was now her husband, but he was busy nodding regally at their guests. The crude word was uttered by his brother, Dev Singham.

Anika briefly recalled being introduced to Dev Singham.

She hadn't noticed much before, but now she saw that Dev Singham looked completely different from his brother. He was glaring at someone who was standing next to her.

Anika turned to look behind her and gasped. Her cousin, Sabitha, stood behind her wearing an ornate gold embroidered sari with minimal jewels. It wasn't her attire that had made Anika gasp—it was her cousin's face.

Sabitha had an obvious purple bruise around the corner of her right eye. She also had a cut next to her lip that was barely healed. She was holding a large golden tray where several guests were placing their monetary gifts. Anika also noticed the dark purple bruises around her wrists.

"You are pathetic if you think you can ever win over me," Sabitha said in a menacing tone. "And next time it won't be your leg, it will be your throat."

It took Anika a couple of seconds to realize that Sabitha was speaking with Dev Singham, and he looked quite ruffled. "Why you—"

"Dev. Go check if our ride is ready." The stern order from Abhay Singham stiffened Dev's back. He nodded and walked away from there. Anika watched as he walked with a noticeable limp.

Just after the last of the guests finished blessing them, Neelambari came up to her.

"I will take my niece to the gods and seek their blessings to provide a Singham heir soon," she declared with a smile.

Everyone gave way to her. Not having a choice, Anika followed.

Neelambari stopped in a relatively secluded nook that had a twenty-foot high sculpture of a god. Seeing Neelambari, a few people who stood there to pray, came towards her, touched her feet, and left.

Anika was shocked by the reverence her aunt had received.

"Don't be so shocked, my dear. My people not only love me, they also treat me like a goddess." She smiled indulgently. "If you play your part right, you will soon receive similar kind of treatment from the Singhams and Prajapatis alike."

Anika decided to remain silent. She knew Neelambari had brought her away from the crowd to say something specific.

"And do you know what that part is?" Neelambari asked with eagerness. "The part is to give an heir to the Singhams, continuing the bloodlines."

Anika ignored her. She was already sick of hearing the same thing over and over again.

Meantime, Neelambari removed a delicate necklace from a velvet box. "This was my favorite. It was custom ordered for my wedding by my fiancé. He said that my eyes shone like the jewels in this necklace." Her aunt's voice was soft and whimsical as though she was lost in the memories. "When you enter the Singham household as a bride, I want you to be wearing this."

Anika just stood like an inanimate object letting her aunt fasten the diamond necklace around her neck. "You look radiant, my dear." There was a tinkling laugh. "Your husband will look beyond his hatred for the Prajapatis and take you tonight. Don't fight him. And even if it hurts because you are a virgin, and are not used to a man's touch, remember, it is your duty to submit to him and present him with an heir."

Anika's heart thudded as she heard the words. "How do you know?" she asked.

"Know what?"

"Whether or not I am a virgin."

There was a pause and a delicate shrug. "I know because I made sure of it," Neelambari replied. "I made sure you remained pure by not allowing any of those boys to touch what is rightfully Abhay Singham's."

Anika could not believe what she was hearing. "What are you talking about?"

Neelambari watched her with an affectionate smile. "Have you ever wondered why you stayed a virgin despite possessing beauty similar to mine?" she asked. "You were destined to be a Singham bride. I took it up as my duty to ensure that no other boy dared to come in between your destined union."

Anika's head started to spin, and she pressed her fingers into her temple unable to believe her ears. Every date and the hurried break-ups that followed flashed in front of her. The answer to why things had gone south with all her past relationships became clear at that moment.

"You are a sick woman," Anika whispered in shock.

"I did it for your own good. High born, powerful men value virginity. And besides, I wasn't going to take any chances for some random mongrel to plant his bastard in your belly. Your womb should only carry the Singham bloodlines." She laughed at Anika's shocked look. "It's getting late. Let's get back. Your husband must be eager to get started on the first heir."

Anika felt nausea well up within her.

"Cheer up, my love. The next time I meet you, I hope the circumstances are different, and you don't look horrified at the thought of your husband. Oh and by the way... your parents and sister are doing good...for now."

Anika heard the underlying threat, and also the unspoken words, of risking harm to her family, if she didn't toe the line set by Neelambari.

CHAPTER TWELVE

The drive to the Singham Estate was a blur. The roads were bumpy, and each time a pothole caused her to bump into the man sitting next to her, she began trembling and cringing away from him..

The roads got better along the way, and they drove past tall gates which had a large golden carving of a roaring lion's face. Several people watched as she was escorted into what people referred to as a mansion. She kept her head down most of the time, not wanting to see any of their faces. She had received enough hostile stares and threats for the day.

She was given a lavish meal inside a heavily-decorated room, after which she was left alone. After a couple of hours had passed, she became restless. She was sick of waiting and feeling like a lamb before the slaughter. So braving it a little, she decided to go out of the room.

She stepped into a corridor and saw no one, but she could hear faint conversations from a room that was at the end of the circular corridor.

She slowly tiptoed towards the voices, and waited outside, listening in.

"You beat a woman?" She heard Abhay Singham's deep voice thundering at someone.

"She's not a woman!" The other man's voice contained anger and outrage. "Sabitha Prajapati is a crazy psychopath who started it all. She attacked me, and things got out of control, and she ultimately stabbed me in my leg!"

"Why would she attack you?"

There was a chuckle. "Sabitha Prajapati fancies you, big brother. Last night she sent a message, inviting you to come alone to discuss security and something personal, apparently. I was suspicious and went there in your place. She'd planned to seduce you, probably to convince you to marry her instead. Unfortunately for her, I caught her in the act and...she attacked me."

There was a loud noise of smashing and banging something against a table. "I'm sick of hearing about you two. And this is not the first time!"

"But she..."

"She's family now whether we like it or not."

"You can't take her side. You are my brother!"

"I'm on your side, but I also married her cousin. There will be several instances you'll have to see her and interact with her. So trying to kill each other will not get us closer to what we want to accomplish here."

"But I hate her!"

"Then fucking pretend. No one is asking you to like her, but if you mess up our plans, I'll kill you myself."

There was a sullen silence. "Fine. Whatever." There was the sound of a chair being dragged. "So tell me, dear brother. What do you think of Anika Prajapati?"

There was a pause. "What about her?"

There was a chuckle. "You know, you should have read the file I had an investigator prepare about her."

"As I said before, I give a shit. She is just a means to an end."

There was amused laughter. "I believe you. I recall you saying you'd marry her even if she were the ugliest woman in the world."

"You already know what is at stake when it comes to marrying her."

"True, but I just find it incredibly amusing you were prepared for an ugly hag whereas Anika Prajapati turned out to be..." There was a loud whistle.

"I still give a shit about how she looks," an irritable reply came. "As long as she follows my orders, she can do whatever the hell she wants."

"Huh. Knowing the track record of Prajapati women, I somehow doubt it."

"If she doesn't listen, then I'll have to simply get rid of her, and make it look like an accident. Our people will understand, especially if I were to marry the Senani girl next."

Listening to that, Anika trembled. She turned and ran away from there. She was almost hyperventilating when she reached her room.

Abhay Singham was a monster!

My god! How am I going to survive this place?

As soon as she went inside, she shut the double doors, and stood with her back to the doors, catching her breath. Until then, she hadn't realized the possibility of her falling into the fire from a frying pan.

Her body shivered at the new revelation. She had thought everything she had experienced and witnessed at the Prajapati Estate had been her worst nightmare, but this topped it all. If she didn't do as her supposed husband ordered, she would be killed, and her death meant the death of everyone she loved.

Gathering whatever leftover courage she had, and ignoring the heavily decorated king-size bed on a raised dais, she walked to the far end of the room, where a living area was set up with a daybed next to the window. It looked comfortable enough, and also safe enough.

She slowly lay on her side, giving in to the overpowering need to rest, and be lost in a state of denial. As she delved into sleep, she just hoped she wouldn't have a repeat of the nightmares.

*****

Anika slowly began to gain consciousness. She had been in such a deep sleep, she still felt groggy and confused. It was dark, and she was suspended in the air, and moving towards the large king-sized bed. Her heart began to thud as she realized someone was carrying her.

She gasped out as her body hit a soft mattress.

"You will not sleep anywhere else apart from this bed. Do you understand?" the man's deep voice demanded.

She didn't move. She shrunk away from him, and curled up her body tightly, expecting him to hurt her.

"We are married. If you don't behave accordingly, it will not end well for you. You will stay here until I order otherwise."

She shut her eyes tightly ignoring his words and willing her mind to sink back into darkness.

"Answer me!" he roared.

Her body trembled. "Okay," she whispered.

She continued to keep her eyes shut as she heard him move around the room and felt the mattress dip as he slipped into the bed next to her. She braced herself expecting a hand to grab her close, to brutally violate her, while claiming to take what was his by legal right.

But the hand never came.

After a lot of tensed moments, she heard the man's breathing deepen. Only then did her terrified mind relax to be able to slip into an uneasy sleep.

CHAPTER THIRTEEN

Anika slowly opened her eyes, but didn't dare to move. She took in her surroundings with her senses. Everything seemed to be surprisingly calm except for the slow hum of an air conditioner.

Her eyes slowly adjusted to the darkness as the last memory came to her in a flash.

The man had carried her to his bed, and the fragrant petals she smelled, confirmed she was on the same bed that was decorated for the wedding night.

She pulled the edge of the blanket over her ears, desperately wondering if there was anyone in the house she could get help from.

Help for what? To stay alive?

She took a deep breath refusing to let the fear consume her again. Her mind threw in different ideas of escaping, but she knew the moment she was found missing, her crazy aunt would have no mercy on her family.

She lay on her side, barely moving a muscle as she re-played the events over the past few days. A slight movement followed by a ruffling sound brought her out of the haze of the night.

She froze in cold fear when she realized the man she feared the most was only a few feet away from her. She shut her eyes, and held her breath, pretending to be asleep. She lay still until the early hours of the morning, unable to go back to sleep due to the fear of the unknown.

An alarm went off while the sun had barely risen. She heard the man getting up, and moving around the room. She heard the sound of typing on a keyboard, and later there was a scrape of a chair. A door opened and then shut.

After what seemed like only a few minutes, she heard the man return and walk past the bed. There was a sound of a heavy door opening.

The cool morning breeze blew over her, making her burrow into the bedding even more. A constant and continuous whirring sound of some kind filled up the next thirty minutes. Then a little later, there were masculine grunts as something was being systematically punched.

The punching stopped, and she heard the footsteps return to the room. She held her breath when the footsteps sounded louder as they approached the bed.

There was no sound or movement of any kind. The tense silence made her tremble deep inside. She tried to relax by staying still and regulating her breathing.

"If you are done pretending to be asleep, I need to talk to you." The man's deep voice resonated in her ears, making her shudder.

She wanted to ignore him, but if she had to stay alive, she needed to follow his orders. She slowly opened her eyes and looked into the dark eyes that threatened to make her have a nervous breakdown. "I-I wasn't pretending. I just wanted to stay out of your way."

There was silence.

Then his nostrils flared. "I know you didn't want to get married to me, but it's too late. You better accept the situation now."

"I-I don't want to be your wife."

"Too bad. You *are* already my wife, and what you saw outside the Singham temple is the way of life here. Accept it," he growled out.

"I want to...I..." She lost her voice when he crossed his arms in front of his broad chest waiting for her to complete.

Something flickered in his eyes, but it was gone before she could decipher it. "You need to follow every order I pass here. You have no choice, and there are no exceptions."

She nodded, looking down at the pattern on the blanket.

"Look at me when I talk to you." It was a demand, and she obeyed instinctively. "Do not go out. Remain inside until I take you with me. And when I do, you will not utter a word about your family to anyone. Never discuss anything about the families. Do you understand?"

"Yes."

"You will sleep next to me on my bed and not elsewhere like you tried to do last night." His voice was deep and gruff, making her shiver constantly with fear.

"Okay." She felt the burn behind her eyes as she accepted whatever the man was throwing at her like she was a meek mouse. She hated herself at that moment. She hated what the circumstances were turning her into.

"I also don't want a repeat of your performance from yesterday morning before the wedding. If you damage anything deliberately, I'll teach you a lesson that'll make you regret your tantrums." His eyes bore into hers.

"It wasn't a tantrum. I was being forced and... I don't even know you."

There was another eerie silence. "It's already done. You are a Singham now."

Everything inside her rebelled at those words, but she held her tongue.

"Even though I trust my people to an extent, I don't want you to trust anyone except Dev or me."

She stared at him blankly, not understanding what he meant. There was no way she could trust anyone, not even her own so-called family in India, let alone her new husband.

"Do you understand that?" he snapped, making her jump, and nod vigorously.

"Stop being so jumpy, it's annoying," he growled.

Before she could respond, he turned away and disappeared into the bathroom.

She lay back on the bed and closed her eyes. She was fighting tears when she heard him return and move around the room. Was this going to be her life if she ended up being stuck here forever? A meek wife to an indifferent, cruel man she was bound to for life?

No! She refused to give up. She had to find a way out of this mess.

She heard the door shut behind him, on his way out. She got down slowly from the bed and stood on her shaking legs. The traditional outfit she wore felt like a cactus field. The first thing she wanted to do was to get out of it, burn it, if possible. She went straight into the bathroom and shut the door. She cursed when she realized that there was no lock on the door, not that a lock would make her feel any safer.

She turned on the faucet to fill the tub in the massive bathroom, and slid into the water. Her skin felt the relief from the warm water, but her muscles remained tensed.

How long did she have before the man decided to start forcing her on their marital bed to make her conceive?

Fear gripped her body, making her tremble at the prospect of spending her days being hurt, body and soul.

Almost an hour of soaking didn't help relax her muscles. She washed off the soap and reached for a towel wrapping it around her body. She was drying her damp hair with another towel when she heard a sound outside.

She gasped when the bathroom door flew open, and the man stood still, filling the frame. She froze as her mind went blank. She wanted to scream, but she was too scared to do anything.

Moments passed, and then the man took a few steps towards her, making her grip her towel as her lifeline.

He came to a stop, only a foot away from her, and raised his arm, making her flinch and shut her eyes.

"I told you to stop being so jumpy," he growled making her look at him again.

She wanted to shout back at him, asking him to stop being scary, but she could not.

His hand moved past her, reaching for something behind her on the vanity. It was a sleek phone, and he had forgotten it on the counter.

He turned around without another word and was gone leaving her shaking and shivering.

*****

After several minutes, when she was sure he was gone, she stepped out of the bathroom. She pulled out the first things she could reach in her bags and threw them on quickly.

Her stomach rumbled at the smell of food. She had no appetite due to her nervousness and fear. Then she reminded herself that she needed the energy for her brain to come up with a good plan.

She followed the aroma of the food to a small dining nook within the suite. The food was placed on a wheeled cart. Wondering who had brought the cart in, she lifted the covers. Then without even noticing what the breakfast was, she devoured most of it.

She also wondered why the person who had brought the food didn't wait to introduce themselves. Maybe it was another warning for her to stay in the room, and not interact with anyone.

The man had not only ordered her to stay, but also warned her of the consequences.

What would he do if she broke his rules? Beat her? No, not beat her. She recalled his conversation with his brother about hitting a woman. He may not hit her, but he was not opposed to the idea of killing her if she disobeyed. Apparently, for the man she was married to, killing a woman was supposedly better than hurting her.

She shuddered. She could not risk being killed, trying to escape, because that would risk the life of her loved ones.

Feeling defeated, she stood up to explore the large master bedroom suite which was almost as big as her apartment back home.

She walked around cautiously, noticing a corner with a sleek laptop. The man had spent time earlier that morning, typing something.

She sat at the desk and turned on the laptop.

She knew her aunt was probably watching her every move, and maybe even had spies at this place. And if she attempted to warn her family, Neelambari would know immediately.

The laptop screen displayed a single profile. It simply said Abhay Singham. She clicked on it, but to her disappointment, it was password protected.

Frustrated, she looked around the desk, and noticed a stack of books, lined neatly on a bookshelf on one side. She reached for one of them, hoping to find some solace within the pages.

She was an avid reader, and could spend days reading just about anything if she had the time. But lately with her long shifts at the hospital, she missed reading.

She picked out a few more books on random from the shelf and walked towards the balcony. Opening the door, she settled into one of the chairs, and delved into the book, hoping the book would take her mind off her reality.

She heard the door of the suite open and realized it was lunch time. She placed the book on a side table and rushed into the suite. A woman was just about to leave after having placed a wheeled cart with dished on top.

"Wait!"

At her urgent voice, the woman stopped and turned. Seeing the look of utter loathing on the woman's face, Anika's voice died. The woman turned away and left the room.

The same woman brought in snacks and dinner later that day, and her expression and attitude remained the same.

Each time Anika tried to make eye contact or greet her somehow, it was met with an angry silence. Dejected, she lost hope in making the woman her ally.

Finishing her dinner early, she placed the books back in their original places. It was only eight in the evening, but she went to bed early, wanting to avoid any confrontation with the man who was supposedly her husband.

CHAPTER FOURTEEN

Anika woke up slowly from a deep sleep. She was having a pleasant dream. An involuntary purr escaped her as she felt warmth envelop her. She heard a deep masculine groan under her, followed by calloused fingertips tracing the bare curve of her hips.

Why were the fingertips calloused? Being a doctor, and having friends and family who were also mostly doctors, she always shook hands with people who had soft skilled hands that performed surgeries.

She snapped her eyes open, and lifted her head, and then froze as soon as her eyes met with the darkly intense eyes of the man.

She was lying on top of him.

Long moments of silence passed between them as they looked at each other. Her eyes widened with shock and fear, while his were coolly contemplating. Frantically, she tried to move away from his body, but he held her in a firm grip.

"L-let me go," she pleaded, her voice coming out hoarse. Anika realized that lately, her stuttering was coming back more often. It had taken years and several sessions of speech therapy during her childhood to get rid of it. But sometimes, when she was incredibly stressed, it came back.

The man didn't reply. His hand continued to stroke her back, causing tremors to run through her body. The tremors were due to fear, and also due to an unwanted ache deep inside, from the lingering dream.

"I-I don't want this. You know that and yet..."

His large hand paused, and she felt the warmth of it seep deep inside making her body vibrate. His eyes flared, and she didn't know whether it was with lust or anger or both.

"What makes you think I would let anything, including you, stop me from claiming what is rightfully mine?" he inquired dispassionately.

She drew in a long breath, trying to think through the panic that was threatening to take over. "I'm sure a man like you is too proud to force an unwilling woman." She mentally crossed her fingers, desperately hoping her words would hit his ego.

His large hand resumed with the stroking, making her belly quiver with fear, and something else she decided to analyze later.

"Unwilling woman, yes, but not a willing one who crawled on top of me and began burrowing into my neck."

Her face heated in response to his words. She knew she was a restless sleeper and moved a lot during her sleep. "I'm unwilling," she whispered.

"Nothing about you seems unwilling, especially the way you moaned at my touch." He stared at her in an unnerving manner. "I can make your body willing and begging for me in no time."

"That'll still make it wrong because in my mind, I don't want you."

His hands tightened on her hips, making her gasp. Then he moved his hands away from her, and folded them under his head. He stared at the ceiling. "Get off me," he ordered quietly.

Immediately, she scrambled away from him, and got off the bed, and ran into the large bathroom. She was out of breath when she shut the door.

*****

Abhay Singham watched his wife, as she ran away from him. She was breathtaking to look at and also touch, but she had the personality of a frightened deer. She was always trembling. She had been trembling when he had spoken to her for the first time in the Prajapati Estate. She had trembled while she sat next to him during their wedding, and then on the ride to the Singham Estate. She had also been trembling during the two nights while she slept next to him.

Is that all she would do if I touched her the way I want to? Tremble?

The thought filled him with an uncomfortable mix of hate and lust.

*****

Anika slowly looked towards the main bedroom area to check if the man had left. She had heard the sound of a door shut, but she didn't want to take any chances. She had been hiding in the breakfast nook, keeping away from the man as he went about his morning routine.

Taking small, tentative steps, she checked the balcony and then the bathroom.

All clear.

She sighed out a breath of relief, and sped towards the laptop. She tried a few more passwords, but none of them worked.

Frustrated, she got up from the chair to pull out a few more books. The kind of books she had discovered the previous day was more than eclectic.

She couldn't figure out what kind of man she was dealing with simply based on those books.

She ran her fingers along the spine of the books, reading the titles, checking to see which one could take her mind away from constant fear and worry. Her hand stopped when she encountered a soft, leather-bound book with no title. There was one other similar book right next to it.

She pulled the first one out and opened it. She was taken aback when she saw a handwritten text, instead of the print. She held it closer, and squinted at the text, to confirm it was someone's handwriting. The only thing that gave the beautiful calligraphy away was the slightly yellowed pages, and the tiny ink blots.

"...I stood in front of my brothers, holding the bloodied birds I had shot. I had proven to them that I was a proud Senani woman who is more than capable of accompanying them to the hunts..."

Anika closed the book and bit her lip, feeling guilty. It was someone's journal.

But whose? And the name Senani sounded familiar. Feeling curious and equally guilty, she opened the journal again.

"...mother was upset. She wanted me to spend more time learning about running a large estate to be a worthy bride to Abhimanyu Singham..."

Anika sucked in a breath. The word Singham jumped out at her, pushing away all the guilt. Her heart thudded as she decided to continue reading it. Holding the book carefully, she went to the balcony, and settled into one of the chairs.

CHAPTER FIFTEEN

A television was playing in the background.

Wait, there was no television in the room.

It had been only a week since Anika arrived at the Singham Estate, but it felt more like eons. Over the week, she had become used to the bedroom suite. Even though the original building was probably built hundreds of years ago, the interiors kept up with the modern times. At least, the master bedroom suite appeared to have been updated in the recent times. The suite had a dedicated area for each function, giving her some space even when *he* was around.

She opened her eyes as slits, and saw the man at his work desk with his headphones on. He appeared to be very involved in the telephone conversation. He didn't bother turning towards her, when she got off the bed and walked right past him to the bathroom. She had found the phone call out of the ordinary, because for a change he was talking in long sentences. She had heard him speak on the phone, during the nights, with only single word or curt orders.

She could hear him from the bathroom as he spoke in deep tones in what appeared to be a British accent. His language was fluent, and his tone was well modulated.

Had he taught himself the language by listening to some videos and by reading the books she had found in his room? Or maybe he had a British tutor brought in.

Stepping closer to the bathroom door, she tried to follow his conversation. It was a business conversation, and his voice held obvious authority. She stood close to the door, unable to contain her curiosity.

He seemed to be talking about an agricultural process. Her ears perked up when she heard a few familiar terms. He was speaking about a prototype product he had planted.

A few minutes into the conversation, she felt guilty for eavesdropping, but a moment later she brushed it off. This was for her survival and possibly her family's survival, too.

She couldn't believe he kept her trapped in this room for more than a week. Each time he left for the day, she had to stop herself from getting out of the room.

The strong push from the other side of the door brought her out of her thoughts. She almost fell on the bathroom floor when it opened suddenly. She stumbled but held the edge of a countertop on time. She shrunk away from him.

"What are you doing?" he asked with a frown.

Her mind went blank, and she didn't know how to answer that question. "I-I..."

He waited for her answer with an impatient look. And looking at his scowling face, she felt even more nervous, and cowered over the counter.

"What is wrong with you?" he asked in disgust. "Why are you hiding inside the suite all day? There is a rumor floating around with the Prajapatis that I might have murdered you on our first night."

Her legs trembled when she heard the word murder. "B-but you told me I had to stay here in the room."

His frown deepened. "When?"

"On the first night."

He stilled, and then shook his head briefly. "I have no time for this. Get out of the room and do whatever the hell you want within reason."

Her heart leaped, and she nodded her head. She slowly stood straight, calculating the path to escape from the bathroom without touching him.

He stared at her for a few more moments, his eyes scanning her body like he was contemplating his next move. She caught her breath waiting for him to do something—like pounce on her or grab her. But he didn't do any of those things. With another look of disgust, he turned away from her and went towards the exercise area.

She began to hear the loud punching noises where he beat the crap out of a punching bag.

*****

Zipping through the shower, Anika pulled out a semi-traditional tunic and leggings for her first outing. Her mind was preoccupied with hundreds of thoughts bombarding her at the same time.

Who else lived in the house?

The only relative of his seemed to be his brother.

But there were a lot of other people who had waited for them outside the main door of the Singham house on the wedding day.

Was there at least one person out there who would help me?

She recalled overhearing a conversation the man had on the phone, with his brother. The man was asking his brother to go back to the city. It wasn't clear why the brother wanted to stay, even though the man had wanted him to leave immediately.

Gathering up the courage she could muster, she opened the bedroom door to step outside. The only time she had wandered around the Singham Mansion was after the wedding. Now, she didn't know where to go first.

Just as she was about to close the door, her eyes fell on the finished breakfast that sat on the small dining table within the suite. She stepped back inside to gather the dishes, and carried them on the tray, on her way out.

A long breath didn't help, but she took her first step towards relative freedom.

She was on the top level of the house. A circular corridor led to the stairs. She walked to the railing and looked up to see the source of light. There was a magnificent oil painting on the skylight that was large enough to illuminate the entire interior of the house.

She slowly looked down and saw a couple of men stationed at the bottom of the staircase. Were they guarding her so she couldn't escape? If only they knew that running away wasn't an option for her. Her aunt wouldn't think twice before harming her family the moment she found out.

There were a few other people on the second floor, cleaning and polishing the marble floors. A few of them were moving around, holding things in their hands. She continued walking down the stairs tentatively smiling at every person she saw. They were all looking at her, but none of them returned her smile.

Keeping her back straight, she reached the bottom of the stairs.

"Which way to the kitchen?" she asked one of the men, her voice wobbling only slightly.

One of the men reached out to take the tray of dishes from her, but she shook her head. "I'll take it. The kitchen?"

"Seventh door to the right." The man pointed in the general direction.

She walked along the corridor, drawing glances from people passing by.

What if no one here ever likes me enough to help me?

Her nervousness came back, and her palms started to get sweaty, making her worried about dropping the tray before she made it to the kitchen.

She stepped into a large room, where over a dozen women were working. They were cutting, prepping the food, and even cooking on several burners of multiple stoves. Anika recognized the woman who usually brought her food up to the bedroom.

When the women noticed her presence, no one uttered a word, filling the air with a tense silence. Fighting the instincts to run out of the room, Anika braced herself and kept walking.

Her steps resounded in the over-sized kitchen. Slowly she placed the tray on a granite counter, before turning to look at the woman who brought her food each day.

Anika smiled tentatively. "Thank you for bringing my meals to the room. I don't need them brought in anymore. I'll join everyone else."

The tense silence was getting thicker, and she didn't know why everyone looked at her with cold, hostile faces.

What had she done to anger them?

Finally, a woman spoke. She came closer and gave a sweeping derisive look. "Look who decided to finally step out of her room!"

Anika smiled uncomfortably, not knowing what to say. How was she supposed to tell them that she wasn't staying in her room by choice? That would only make her sound like a liar. Based on what the man had said to her that morning, she realized she might have misunderstood his words.

She cleared her throat. "I'm just here to see if I can help in any way."

"You think you can take over the house, and rule all of us, just because you are married to Abhay?" the woman hissed.

Anika was taken aback by the sudden unwarranted attack. "I just wanted to drop off the dishes and meet the people here," she answered quietly.

"Don't pretend. You are still a Prajapati woman. Abhay *had* to marry you for his people!"

Anika frowned trying to process her words.

"Don't try to pretend as though you know nothing! You can't fool us. We know how the Prajapatis are, and you are definitely one of them." The woman spat out the words.

Anika wanted to shout back at the woman, telling her that she didn't know anything about what went on between the Prajapatis and Singhams. But she held herself back because she was here to make allies, not enemies.

However, everyone looked as though they couldn't wait to see her suffer or just die.

"I just wanted to meet everyone in the house," she reiterated to their hostile faces.

"Don't try to fool us with your harmless demeanor. We know what the Prajapatis are capable of!" The woman's voice held a lot of anger and also traces of hurt.

Anika knew she wasn't going to magically change people's attitude towards her. So she didn't waste her time or energy trying to make them understand that she was not out to harm them in any way.

Her shoulders stooped in defeat as she walked out from the kitchen. She went towards the main door, determined to find someone outside, who was ready to speak to her in a friendly tone.

The woman who had been shouting at her followed her out of the kitchen. "Where do you think you are going? How dare you move about like it's your own home?"

"I just wanted to see outside."

"The Singham Mansion is not your home. It does not belong to a Prajapati!"

"This is her home. She is a Singham now." The deep, chilling voice that interrupted them, made Anika freeze. It sounded so much like Abhay Singham's voice, but she didn't have to turn to know it wasn't him. She had spent too much time over the past week staying inside her luxurious prison, simply listening to him while she closed her eyes, pretending to be asleep.

"Dev... I was just... her family is the reason..." The woman's voice trailed off.

"Do you have any idea what Abhay would do if he found out you are talking about the families and the feud?"

Anika slowly turned to look. The man who spoke was Dev Singham. She had seen him on the day of her wedding, and also heard him speak the night when she had eavesdropped on the conversation between him and his brother.

The woman kept arguing, refusing to give up. "You know why Abhay married her, Dev! But she is acting as though she is a cherished bride and not our enemy. She is trying to take over this house and all of us. She might even spy on us to give information to Prajapati. They'll attack and murder us in our homes—"

"Malini, one more word, and it won't be Abhay who'll kill you.I will." Dev's voice, although dead calm, held a lot of menace. Instead of being scared of Dev as she did with his older brother, Anika found his defense of her encouraging. *Could Dev be an ally?*

Malini was watching Dev with a sulky yet scared look. She threw another look of hatred towards Anika before walking away.

"Thank you, Dev." Anika smiled tentatively, not knowing what to expect from Dev Singham.

Dev's expression changed instantly. From the cold menace, his face transformed to a friendly one with an easy smile. "Don't worry about what Malini says. It'll take time for our people to get used to you."

They are not my people.

"It's okay, I understand," she said, even though she had no clue why the people in the Singham household were angry.

"You will understand them slowly, Anika, but make sure you don't tolerate disrespect from any of them. Let Abhay or me know if anyone speaks to you in that tone again."

Her heart thumped as she heard those words. Dev sounded like a logical person who understood people and respected them. He really could be her ticket to freedom.

"Are you going out?" she asked. She saw he was wearing a business suit. It looked odd against the various antiques and also the tall intricate carvings of the Singham house. No not house... mansion.

Dev smiled. "Yes. I'm heading back to the city. Boss's orders."

"Boss?"

He laughed. "At least he behaves like my boss most of the time. I'm sure you already discovered by now that Abhay is quite bossy."

Anika didn't return the smile. She couldn't, even though she tried to force herself.

Anika didn't find her situation amusing. She was being threatened, more or less at gunpoint by Neelambari. Each day Anika worried and feared for her family. And each night, she suffered from worry and fear for herself. She was worried she would be raped by her husband who either threw orders at her, or behaved like he was disgusted by her.

Dev looked at her face and ran his fingers through his hair. "My brother is not that bad, Anika. You'll get used to him," he said softly.

She nodded. "Dev... before you go. Can you tell me where is the library?"

Dev broke into another easy smile. "Wow, another bookworm! My brother was the only one in this house until now." He laughed in amusement. "You'll find the library on the same floor as your suite. I'll send someone to escort you."

"Thank you."

"Pleasure is all mine, Anika," he said. "And welcome to the Singham family. I guess I'll see you in a few weeks. So take care and send out a word to me if you need anything."

At his offer, she broke into a genuine smile.

Waving a goodbye to her, he left.

A couple of moments later, a uniformed man came towards her and escorted her to the library. She slowly walked into the library, staring at the rows and rows of books that lined the almost forty-feet-high walls.

Oh shit. How am I supposed to find the rest of the journals here?

She spent the next three hours just looking through the catalogs with the list of books. She had to find the remaining parts of the journal that she had been reading, since the previous week. It was written beautifully by a woman named Devasena, who was married to a Singham.

Devasena was a well-educated person, and she led a fascinating life. The first journal and almost three-fourths of the second one as well, contained the details of the Devasena's girlhood adventures. Devasena was one of the outliers who was trying to make her mark in the obviously male-dominated household. Towards the end of the second journal, details about Devasena preparing to marry a man she had never met were written evocatively.

Anika could not understand why Devasena was looking forward to marrying a man she had never met, purely for the sake of family duty. Devasena had also written about how her would-be husband had a reputation for being brutal, while invoking swift justice.

Just reading about Abhimanyu Singham and his deeds was terrifying. But for some reason, Devasena had written about his brutal acts as though they were something to be proud of. The journal ended the night before Devasena and Abhimanyu's wedding.

Anika was desperate to find the next volumes. Devasena's situation seemed so similar to hers when it came to marrying strangers who led a violent and brutal life, yet the feelings they had towards their respective husbands was vastly different.

"Tomorrow, I will be married to Abhimanyu Singham. I feel blessed by the chance given to me to secure the prosperity of the lands for generations to

come. *I will stand next to the man who has been destined to me through the hundred-year-old tradition. Together we will serve and protect our people. I will be Devasena Singham tomorrow.*"

Anika felt the enthusiasm and eagerness that Devasena had felt towards her marriage.

Did Devasena lead a happy life? Or was she killed shortly by her brutal husband after the marriage?

Anika badly wanted Devasena to be okay.

CHAPTER SIXTEEN

Anika was still going through the list of library books in the dozens of catalogs spread around her, when she felt a prickling sensation on her neck. She looked up and her eyes met with an angry pair.

"Why are you hiding here since this morning?" Abhay Singham demanded.

"I-I like to read." It had to be very late at night if he was back.

He threw the book in his hand on a chair next to her. "You were supposed to spend time outside, so people know you are still alive."

"I tried." She mumbled the words.

"And?"

"They said...they weren't...I mean...they... they..." Anika's tired brain wasn't able to process, how to let him know in a diplomatic manner, that his people hated her, and didn't want to deal with her.

He loomed on top of her with a thunderous frown as he waited for an answer from her.

Luckily there was a knock on the door that interrupted them.

"Abhay!" A strained female voice called out to him, visibly shifting his expression. His frown morphed into alertness, and he strode out of the room. For reasons she couldn't explain, she followed him out of the library.

He went down the stairs, towards the ground floor, where a group of people had gathered. People parted as he neared, and Anika could see a small girl lying on the floor wheezing.

One look at the girl's splotchy, red face, Anika knew what was happening. Knowing there wasn't a lot of time, she ran back upstairs, towards the bedroom and straight into the closet where her suitcases were.

She pulled her medical pouch out of one of her bags and rushed out, clutching it as she ran down the stairs.

By the time she made it downstairs, the girl was coughing, and her skin was turning blue.

Anika pulled out the liquid medication from the pouch. She pushed aside the people who were trying to make the girl drink more water. A few of them resisted, but she pulled the glass of water from their hands and poured it on the floor. "Stop, and move aside. She is having an allergic reaction."

Not bothering to wait for their reactions, she measured the medication and poured it into the girl's mouth. "Swallow," she told the girl in a calm, gentle voice.

The girl looked at her and then tried to swallow the medication. But the look on her face made it clear that she was unable to swallow. With the next hacking cough, the medication spewed out.

"What are you giving her?" A voice of a woman demanded. "Are you trying to kill her?"

Anika recognized the voice from this morning. It was the same woman who had taunted her earlier that day. Murmurs grew around them, but Anika ignored them. She filled up the medicine into an inhaler and placed it over the girl's mouth. When the girl began to breathe, Anika looked at the people hovering too close.

"Move back. She needs some fresh air."

She hoped the girl would be able to breathe freely soon, but her symptoms seemed to be getting worse. She checked the girls pulse, and it was dropping.

"We need an ambulance, now!" Anika told the people. She looked around frantically and saw Abhay Singham standing a few feet away, yelling into his phone.

The girl's coughs grew weaker, prompting Anika to pull out an adrenaline shot from the pouch. She grew up with severe food allergies, and knew exactly what the girl was going through.

"She is going to kill our Meena," someone in the background cried, but Anika ignored the remarks. She knew what she was doing. She adjusted the girl's sleeve and drove the needle into the shoulder, releasing the medication.

"Breathe," she told the girl. "You'll be fine in a few minutes." She pulled out the second shot, just in case the first one didn't work immediately. She placed the inhaler to the girl's mouth, watching her closely, and feeling relieved to see the girl's skin returning to a normal color.

People began to hover over the girl again. "Please, step back. She needs air."

For a change, the people around complied, but she felt someone closing in on her again, and standing right next to her. "I said she needs to breathe! Move away!" She placed a hand on a leg, and pushed a little, but the person didn't budge.

When she looked up, her eyes met with Abhay Singham's. Her palm froze on him for a moment before she jerked her hand back.

"The doctor will be here in a minute," he stated calmly.

"S-she will be fine. She just had an allergic reaction, most likely food allergy."

Abhay turned to one of the elderly women who was standing next to the girl by her feet. "Did Meena eat anything new today?"

"No," replied the woman.

"What did she eat?" Anika asked.

"She ate prawn curry and started coughing a few minutes later."

Anika frowned. "Are they farmed or sea caught?" she asked.

"Farmed," Abhay replied quietly. "I think I know why she had this reaction."

Before Anika could ask him to explain, an older man carrying a bag, hurried towards the girl. "How is she?" he asked.

Anika saw him remove a stethoscope from his case.

The older woman began to explain what had happened with the child. She also mentioned that Anika had helped.

The doctor smiled Anika. "Thank you for helping," he said. "Have you read about dealing with allergic reactions?"

"Yes."

"That's great. I could use a lot of help here. I'm always short of people who are willing to help the injured or the sick. Maybe I can train you with some basic emergency techniques if you are interested."

"No. That's not necessary," Anika replied.

"Oh." The doctor's face fell. "I thought you would be interested. Abhay always helped when required, and I thought... "

Anika shook her head. "No, I meant the training is not necessary, Dr. Rao. I'm already qualified."

"Oh." Dr. Rao's eyes lit up. "Do you happen to be a nurse by chance?"

"No. I'm a—" Anika broke off when she saw Abhay Singham's impassive face.

Tearing her eyes away from the intimidating man's face, she looked at the eager face of the older man. "I'm a doctor. General medicine."

There was a stunned silence in the room.

Then Dr. Rao broke into an excited grin. "That is such great news!"

Anika smiled back tentatively.

The doctor's eyes fell on her medical bag, placed on the ground. "So you didn't just give the girl some vapor to ease her breathing?" the doctor asked, looking confused.

"No, I gave her an adrenaline shot." Anika gave him the details about dosage.

"Oh... but how did you have the adrenaline shots handy to give the child?"

"I have food allergies, and sometimes I have similar reactions."

Anika felt Abhay Singham's eyes on her. Until then, while she was dealing with an emergency, she had almost forgotten everything except for saving the girl's life. She was back to the reality as soon as she felt his glare.

Instead of thanking her, Abhay Singham looked pissed at her.

Surprisingly, he directed his pissed-off gaze towards the doctor. "Dr. Rao, does Meena need to go to the hospital?"

"No, she is fine now." The doctor packed up his case and stood up.

"It was my pleasure to meet you, Dr. Singham." The innocent words of the doctor made her wince. *Yikes, is that my new identity?*

"Take Meena inside and send up dinner to the suite," Abhay instructed someone.

He then directed his gaze towards her. "Let's go."

When she stood rooted to the ground, feeling uncertain, his frown grew in size. He grabbed her wrist and tugged her towards him. The grip on her wrist wasn't hard, but she felt the burn as he led her up the stairs to the master bedroom. He shut the door behind them as soon as they were back in the suite.

Anika felt paralyzed when she saw the rage on his face. She cowered, expecting him to lash out at her about something or the other.

"Why didn't you tell me you had food allergies? You could have died if you ate something by accident while I was away."

She was so shocked by the unexpected question and statement, she stopped trembling. "I-I check before I eat anything."

"How?" he demanded.

"I'm only allergic to food color, and I noticed no artificial colors have been used in any of the dishes here."

His frown softened. He was about to say something but stopped when they heard a soft knocking.

"Come in," he said out loud. And then he looked at her. "Have dinner and sleep here and not in the library."

She nodded slowly. He looked at her for a few tense moments before striding out of the room past the woman who was rolling in the food cart.

The woman began to set the dishes on to the dining nook. After she was done, instead of walking away with the cart, she stood up and looked at Anika with a smile on her face.

"My name is Lakshmi. I want to make you your favorite dish tomorrow." The woman smiled sheepishly.

"Thank you, Lakshmi. I liked the beetroot chutney that was made a few days ago. I would love to have some more tomorrow."

Lakshmi smiled again and left.

After dinner and a shower, Anika laid on the bed, staring at the ceiling. So far, she had three potential allies—Dev, Dr. Rao, and Lakshmi. They seemed nice, but she didn't know whether any of them would dare to cross Abhay Singham, to be able to sympathize with her situation and help her.

That meant, apart from building allies, she also needed to work faster on getting her family to safety.

CHAPTER SEVENTEEN

The next morning, when Anika went down to the kitchen, she saw a couple of smiling faces. Tentatively, she smiled back.

"Dr. Singham, where would you like to have your breakfast?"

Anika looked at the girl and recalled seeing her last evening. She had been standing close to the other girl who had the allergic reaction.

"If you don't mind, I'd like to join some of you. That is if you haven't had breakfast already."

The girl's smile widened. "Sure. I'm Sonu by the way. I usually have my breakfast at eight in the garden."

"That sounds great, Sonu. Let me know what I need to carry from here." Anika saw several large dishes laid out on the humungous kitchen island. She hadn't had a chance to explore the mansion yet, but she was looking forward to it.

"Oh no! You don't have to carry it. I can bring them, and we have several helpers who can do it as well."

"I insist." She smiled at the visibly surprised girl.

She wondered why the girl looked so surprised when she insisted on helping. The people in the house addressed the man she was married to, by his name. The people here were considered part of the household rather than help. It was a complete contrast to what she had noticed at the Prajapati household. There was a clear expectation of deference when it came to Neelambari and Sabitha. In fact, she couldn't imagine her aunt or cousin asking their maids and other help to call them by their first names.

Did that mean, the man was not as much of a monster as she expected him to be?

How bad could he be if his people addressed him by his name?

With that thought, her mind eased a little. Picking up the tray with a few dishes placed on top, she followed behind Sonu.

They sat near a part of the garden that offered a spectacular view of a fountain with a large lotus pond. There were other vivid colored flowering plants around it. Combined with the sounds of birds singing, it was very peaceful.

Anika frowned as a thought struck her. "I thought there was a drought. Why is the water being wasted this way?"

"Recycled water... " Sonu answered in between bites. "Water used from the mansion is collected and filtered."

"I see."

Anika didn't know what to think of this place. On the one hand, they believed in curses and superstitions, while on the other hand, they made use of modern technology.

Just as they continued with their breakfast, an old woman appeared next to them.

"I have an indigestion problem," she said.

"Excuse me?" Anika asked.

"I'm not able to move freely or do any work because of it. Can you check me and give me medications for it?"

Anika shook her head. "Sorry. I don't have the equipment or the medications to treat you. You should check with Dr. Rao? He..."

The woman frowned. "No. Dr. Rao is always busy seeing other patients who have life-threatening injuries. I'm sure you can help. You helped Meena last night."

"Yes, but that was..."

"Please. I'm an old woman. I am feeling useless with this stomach irritation. I'm not able to work properly."

"I understand. But..."

"Please."

Anika sighed. "Okay. I might have something in my medical kit. I'll check and give it to you."

"God bless you!"

After the woman left, Sonu and Anika finished their breakfast and took the dishes back to the kitchen.

"Thank you for keeping me company for the breakfast, Sonu. Do you have time to accompany me around the mansion grounds?"

"No problem," said Sonu with a smile. "I'll be off to school now and will be back in the evening. If you wish, I can show you around the mansion grounds during that time. It's beautiful around sunset time."

Anika smiled. "Deal."

After waving goodbye to Sonu, Anika went up to the bedroom to bring the medications to the old woman. She knew the man would be gone by then.

Grabbing the medications, she searched and found the woman waiting near the kitchen. She gave the tablets to her along with the instructions.

She then returned back to the suite. The next couple of hours she spent in frustration trying to guess the password of the computer. Then an idea struck her.

She waited until Lakshmi came up to the suite with her lunch.

"Do you know Dev's number? I need to ask him something."

Lakshmi didn't hesitate and wrote down his number on a piece of paper.

"I don't have a phone. Can I borrow your mobile phone?" Anika asked.

Lakshmi looked surprised. "We don't have mobile towers, just a few satellite phones. I don't have one."

Anika's face fell.

"Malini has one. Let me bring it up to you," said Lakshmi before leaving the room.

Ten minutes later, Anika tapped her foot nervously as the phone began to ring. Dev answered after several rings.

"Dev?"

There was silence on the other end.

"Dev, this is Anika."

"Anika! Sorry I didn't realize you were calling me. How are you?"

Anika took a deep breath, mentally crossing her fingers. "I'm good. I called because I wanted to know if there is a computer I could use. There's one in the room, but I forgot to ask...Abhay...the password." The man's name felt strange on her tongue, and it caused a small shiver to pass through her body.

"No problem," said Dev. "The password is Arundhati. A-r-u-n-d-h-a-t-i. Ask Abhay to get you a phone—"

Dev broke off to speak to someone on his end. Anika could hear him get angry and upset about something. She was about to hang up, thinking he had forgotten about her, but he returned. "Sorry about that. Can I call you back, Anika?"

"That's okay, Dev. I just needed the password. Thanks."

After ending the call, she smiled and handed the phone back to Lakshmi. As soon as the other woman left, Anika locked the room and tried to log into the laptop.

She almost shouted in sheer relief when she was finally able to log in successfully.

Heart pounding, she spent the next two hours in front of the laptop, and then wiped away all the traces of her browsing history.

CHAPTER EIGHTEEN

Over the next week, she began to fall into a pattern. Each morning, she woke up and freshened up before running out of the room for breakfast. After breakfast, she spent time on the computer reaching out to her contacts. Then later, she went to the library browsing through the catalogs.

Whenever she interacted with the people downstairs, some of them came to her with some or other complaints of minor ailments for which they wanted medications. Soon she began to run out of her limited medicines that she carried with her.

One day, while browsing through the catalogs, she found a book on home remedies using herbal medications.

Growing up, even though her mom and stepdad were doctors, whenever she or Myra fell sick, her mom always tried using home remedies to cure minor colds or fevers. Even after becoming a doctor, she also preferred using natural remedies as much as possible.

She browsed through the book and found that it had clear instructions of what remedy could be used for various minor illnesses. The good part about most of the natural medications was—they had no side effects.

Feeling it could be useful to the people living within the Singham Estate, she brought it down with her.

She showed it to the woman who had the stomach problem.

"This is Arundhati's!" an old woman exclaimed.

"Who is Arundhati?" She remembered the password for the computer was the same name.

"Abhay's mother. She was an expert in curing a lot of ailments using natural remedies. Sometimes people queued up from the neighboring villages to get her help."

Anika was disappointed that Devasena wasn't the name of Abhay's mother. Each day, for a couple of hours, she was still obsessively searching for Devasena's journals in the library.

"I see. What happened to her?" Anika placed the question casually, even though she knew she could be in a whole lot trouble if Abhay Singham found that she had been snooping around.

The old woman's eyes fired up. "A lying cheating dog murdered her. That's what happened!"

Anika was shocked. "What do you mean murdered?"

There was pure hatred in the old woman's face. "The dirty lying bastard—"

"Sitamma!" Abhay Singham's angry voice interrupted.

The old woman paled looking at his furious face. Anika felt equally terrified. Over the past week, she had barely interacted or seen him. The moment she woke up, she simply ran out the room to have breakfast and other meals with the rest of the household. During the night, after a long day of helping people and searching the library, she was exhausted enough to almost faint asleep.

And right then, she was back to being terrified of him, especially because he came closer to her, and pulled her away from the people to one of the rooms, and banged the door shut.

"I had warned you before of speaking about our families."

"I-I was just curious to know more about this place and everyone. Please, it's not Sitamma's fault. I asked her who Arundhati was."

He looked even more pissed. "Don't ever discuss her again."

"W-why?" she challenged. She was sick of walking on eggshells around him. "She is your mother which makes her my mother-in-law. I have the right to know everything about her."

His eyes flared as she spoke, and he looked terrifying. He slowly walked towards her and stopped only a few inches away. "Right?" he asked in cold menace.

"Y-yes. I have the right." She fisted her hands to stop them from shaking.

He smiled slowly. With his perfect masculine features and even teeth, he looked dazzlingly handsome from the outside, but all she felt was cold fear at the glint in his eye as he gave her a sweeping appraisal.

"I wanted to give you some time to adjust before you take up your duties as my wife, but if you are so willing and eager to demand your rights, then maybe we should do something about fulfilling all your other wifely duties sooner."

At this threat, she wanted to step away in panic, but she stopped herself. It was time she called his bluff. Everyone at the Singham household worshipped him. How bad could he really be?

"You are not a monster. I know you won't hurt me—"

Before she could finish the sentence, he grabbed her close by her hair and pulled her head back.

She gasped in fear.

"Don't ever assume things about me," he hissed out, tightening the pressure on her hair, causing her to whimper.

"You won't hurt a w-woman," she pressed.

"I am hurting you right now," he said, watching her face with utter loathing. "I have been dreaming of hurting you in ways you wouldn't imagine even a monster to do. Believe me, I'd feel justified, and so will rest of my people. I should be torturing you, ripping out your soul until all that is left is an empty shell. Maybe that will compensate for my loss."

She felt his hands wrap around her neck, tightening the pressure around it. She screamed in fear. The next moment, he dragged the material around her neck towards her stomach, causing a loud rip. The torn top fell around her waist, leaving her almost bare in her bra.

He picked her up like a rag doll, and threw her on the nearby bed, and climbed on top of her.

Her throat froze in utter fear as she watched the glittering dark eyes filled with rage. He stared at her for the longest time, until she felt tears leaking from her eyes.

After several moments of silence, he loosened the grip on her hair.

"Now do you believe I can be a monster?" he asked quietly, causing chills to break out on her skin.

She jerked her head once.

"Make sure you follow my orders. Don't ever ask or discuss anyone's family again," he said.

With her heart thudding, she nodded.

"Give me the words," he demanded.

"I-I won't ask about anyone's family again," she whispered.

"Good."

With that, he rolled away from her, got up from the bed, and left the room, leaving her shaking and trembling.

The rest of the day, she remained frightened. She spent most of her time at the library, continuing her search. A few hours later, she finally found the rest of Devasena's journals—that was the only silver lining to her living nightmare.

CHAPTER NINETEEN

"What's so funny?" Anika asked when the sounds of giggles made her look up.

The two teenage girls continued to giggle.

Anika was in the yard planting medicinal herbs. Meena and Sonu were her usual helpers during the yard work. She had grown rather fond of them in the past few days.

Anika smiled. "Tell me so I can join you girls."

Their giggles broke into laughter as they pointed towards the top of the building.

"Huh?" Anika looked up, and immediately her eyes fell on the tall figure leaning against the balcony wall looking down at them. She felt an unexpected zing pass through her, when their eyes met. The man stared at her for a long moment before gesturing her to go up to him.

She was almost tempted to shake her head no, but she knew that would only lead him to come down to her and drag her upstairs. It would only piss him off more.

"You two stay put and finish up. I will be right back." She dusted her hands and stood up to leave.

When she reached the room, she took a deep breath before entering into the lion's den.

"Close the door," the man said quietly. His back was facing her as he was taking something out of the safe. Despite spending a lot of time in the room, she hadn't realized there was a safe within. She closed the door and turned back towards him. She froze when his eyes were on her muddy shoes.

"Umm... I was working in the yard... " she explained unnecessarily even though he had seen her from the balcony.

He held a large velvet rectangular box in his hands giving her his usual expressionless look. "Wear this to the temple next week."

Carefully, she took the box from his hands and opened it. She gasped looking at the beautiful necklace. She wasn't a jewelry person, but the intricate carving and the precious stones embedded within took her breath away.

She recalled reading in Devasena's journal about the custom of exchanging gifts on the twenty-first day of the wedding, and then also the ceremony they needed to perform at the temple.

Abhimanyu Singham had custom ordered a breathtaking necklace for his wife, and in return, Devasena had gifted him a jeweled hunting knife.

Anika recalled how excited Devasena had felt on that day.

"Thank you," Anika said softly. "But I don't have anything to give to you."

A surprised look passed on the man's stern face for a moment. "I guess I'll survive," he said tonelessly.

Anika compressed her lips to avoid snapping at him. What was she thinking? She had been reading Devasena's journals so much that sometimes she mixed up their worlds. Unlike Abhimanyu Singham who was a fierce yet loving husband, Abhay Singham was just a bullying ass. She had been trying to keep out of his way the entire week, but all she got from him were sneers and more threats thrown into the mix.

"I need you to behave at the temple. I want you to convince everyone this marriage has been consummated, and we are actively working on conceiving an heir. If anyone thinks otherwise, I might have to make it real. Do you understand?"

She hated the thinly veiled threat and bit her lip from stopping herself from lashing out at him.

"Well?" he demanded.

"Yes!" she snapped, unable to keep quiet anymore.

She expected him to say something nasty to frighten her, but surprisingly, his eyes looked amused. "I think I like this version of you better."

After saying those cryptic words, he strode out of the room. Moments later, she heard him barking out orders.

Once his voice completely faded away, she carefully placed the jewelry box on a chest within the closet, and returned to the yard work.

*****

Over the next few hours, she continued planting the herbs based on Arundhati Singham's book. When she was finishing up the last of the plantings, she noticed a lot of buzz outside the house where people were gesturing and talking frantically.

"What's happening?" she asked, looking at some of the tense faces.

"They lit a fire in the warehouse and destroyed most of the grains." An older woman looked devastated.

"Who lit the fire?"

"Those rabid dogs! The Senanis."

Anika's heart jumped when she heard that name. Devasena was a Senani who was married to a Singham. Why were the Singham's and Senanis at war?

"Will the farmer's families suffer because of this?" Anika knew the area already suffered from drought. To have something as precious as grains destroyed would be truly devastating.

"No. Abhay always makes sure that farmers and their families don't suffer. But we all worked so hard, and Abhay had also put in his sweat to grow the drought-resistant crop. It took just a few minutes for the Senanis to destroy the fruits of our hard work."

"I'm sorry," Anika said softly, meaning it. "Let me know if I can help in any way."

The old woman looked at her with a sad smile. "You are kind. You remind me so much of Arundhati. She was also a very kind-hearted woman. Everyone adored her."

Anika was curious, but she stopped herself from asking more. She recalled Abhay Singham's reaction when she had inquired about his mother the last time.

Soon it was dark. Anika went up to her room after dinner. She hadn't been able to spend much time in the library that day due to the yard work. She headed to the bathroom to take a quick shower, but as soon as she stepped into the bathroom, her eyes fell on the large bathtub.

All the minor aches she had acquired due to the yard work that day seemed to twinge at the same time. Sighing, she decided to run a bath knowing the man wasn't going to be back anytime soon. She sprinkled the bath salts into the water, stripped off her clothes, and stepped into the bath.

She groaned as she stepped into the warm water that soothed her sore muscles. The sweet smell of the lavender in the salts transported her to a happy place. She rested her neck against the rounded edge of the tub, and slid lower into the water. Her eyes rolled shut as she relaxed her mind and body.

Moments later, a loud crash stripped her of the brief peace, and she opened her eyes to find Abhay Singham standing at the doorway.

The sight in front of her, made her shrink and recoil in horror. The obvious stains of dried blood were splattered all over his face and clothes.

She tried hard not to scream in fear.

He began to remove his clothes. When he was completely naked, he walked into the shower.

She lay still in the bathtub trying not to give away her presence. But her trembling caused ripples in the water.

His head was bent down as he let the steaming hot water spray on top of him. She couldn't see him clearly through the mist, but she could feel the palpable anger and tension radiating from his body.

"Fuck!" he growled out loud followed by his fist banging onto the glass wall of the shower. He banged it several times making it vibrate with loud sounds threatening to shatter it.

Each time, his hand connected to the glass, she jumped.

Finally, he stopped banging, and all she could hear was the heavy breathing. She quivered, unable to move, her mind frozen with fear.

Just a few hours ago, she thought he was almost human, but now all she saw was a violent monster which brought her crashing back to the reality. Her fear and insecurity choked her while she felt the strong urge to hide underwater as he continued washing away the blood next to her.

After several moments, he stepped out of the shower and wrapped a towel around his hips.

Just before he was about to leave the bathroom, he turned and looked straight into her eyes.

She thought she would almost pass out with fear, but he turned back and strode out of the bathroom, making her break into relieved sobs.

CHAPTER TWENTY

"A true leader should also be brutal when required to maintain peace."

The next morning when Anika woke up, she recalled Devasena's words. She didn't necessarily agree with that statement, but she understood Devasena's perception. Maybe during that time, the laws of the land were different. In current times, a person did not go on a violent rampage simply because the other person was in the wrong.

She heard the whirring sound of the treadmill. Minutes passed, and then she heard a thud followed by a grunt as he punched a bag. She slowly got out of the bed and moved quietly. She tried to peek through the window and gasped at the sight in front of her.

The man was kicking a punching bag. His broad back and long legs were rock solid with powerful muscles, making her realize that if her plan didn't go accordingly, he was strong enough to break her like a toothpick. She watched him for a few more seconds, and moved away from the window to lay back on the bed. She tried hard to convince herself she wasn't scared of him.

Who was she kidding?

She pulled the blanket partially over her face, and went back to the position she was in all night.

He was in the bedroom closet, getting ready, when she finally opened her eyes, and sneaked away into the bathroom. Ten minutes later, she stared at her reflection with disgust.

What the hell are you doing! Do you want to remain here all your life? Do something. Get out there and execute the plan!

With that pep talk, she stepped out of the bathroom. He was buttoning up the cuffs of a long white pristine shirt. She had often seen him in three-piece formal suits, too.

"Are you going to keep staring or will you talk?" His voice was deep and gravely.

She shuddered, but luckily he missed her reaction as his eyes were downcast while he continued to button the cuffs. During the past month, she had observed quite a few things about him.

Abhay Singham was aloof with everyone in the household. No one relaxed when he was around. They feared him quite a lot, but along with that fear, there was also a healthy dose of respect and awe they felt for him. They even kept saying he was a rational man who listened to their requests and helped them as much as he could. Considering that according to him, she was his wife, she supposed she should expect some amount of the same respect when it came to her wishes.

With that thought, she got back her voice that was stuck in her throat.

"I-I wanted to ask you about something since yesterday. I even waited for you last night." Her voice was too soft, but he heard her.

He raised his head, and his intense eyes hit her face as he studied her. His jaw clenched at whatever he observed on her face.

"Then why didn't you?" he gritted out.

"You had blood on you," she whispered.

He raised an eyebrow. "Never saw blood before *Doctor* Singham?" he asked, stressing the doctor.

She bit her lip. "Yes. But not on someone who had just... just..." she trailed off, not wanting to say killed or murdered.

"Well?"

"You looked... upset last night," she whispered.

His mouth twisted. "Do I seem like the cheerful kind the rest of the time?"

The sarcastic comeback sent a faint bolt of irritation through her. "No, I have never seen you smile or laugh, but usually you are not *that* upset or angry."

He sighed as though he was resigned to the fact that he had to listen to what she had to say. He also began massaging his neck while waiting for her to finish.

Feeling a little bold, she moved closer to him. It felt uncomfortable and unnatural, but she had to try. "You...uh...look tired."

"Because I'm tired as hell," he replied gruffly and then looked at her. Slowly his eyes narrowed as he watched her shrewdly. "What do you want? This pretense of giving a damn about me is annoying."

"No, not pretense. I would like to know what you do all day?" she asked, sticking partially to the truth while her genuine curiosity made her even braver.

"What else? Kill and cause mayhem everywhere," he replied nonchalantly.

Her lips trembled, but she pressed them together. The blasted man was deliberately trying to scare her away, and he was almost succeeding.

"You are with a laptop most mornings, and I heard you speak on the phone about funding some technology-related products. I-I know you do other things. Normal things."

He arched an eyebrow and gave her a slow sweeping look. Starting from the top of her hair to the bottom of her feet, lingering for a few seconds on her lips, and also her chest.

His cruel mouth twisted. "Ah. I almost forgot you are a doctor with a sharp brain in that cowardly body."

"There's a lot you don't know about me." She had wanted to snap out, but her voice came out as a croak. "Please, I want to make my life easier here and adjust to this place and you. Tell me more about yourself."

He gave her a long drawn look. "I might not know much about you, my dear wife, but one thing I do know is that you hate my guts, and would give a damn about knowing more about me."

"N-no. I-I don't hate your guts." It took a tremendous effort on her end to say those words because they were a lie.

She did hate Abhay Singham—for marrying her, and for telling and showing everyone that he owned her. He more or less had her trapped in this grim life.

He watched her with a strange glint in his eyes. "Has anyone ever told you that you are a terrible liar?"

Yes. All the time. Her mom, her stepdad, Myra, and even Nathan. People always caught her whenever she lied. That's why she barely lied, but when it came to self-preservation, she needed to do whatever was required of her, to get out of the hellhole.

"N-no. I'm not l-lying. I don't hate y-you. I want to begin adjusting and make my life easy here."

His nostrils flared, and he wrapped his fingers around the nape of her neck and jerked her close. There were only a few inches between their faces.

Her heart thudded so loudly and hard that she thought she'd pass out, but she recalled her resolve. She was done being scared. She needed to come out of the entire debacle with her guns blazing. She winced at the metaphor that was almost a pun.

Abhay Singham's eyes narrowed with suspicion. Then slowly a smile or rather a smirk appeared on his face. "Prove it," he challenged. "Prove to me that you don't hate me or fear me, and that you want to adjust to this life."

"H-how?"

Letting go of her neck, he shrugged. "You were the one who just said you didn't hate me and wanted to adjust. So show me."

She stood with an uncertain look causing a gleam to appear in his eyes.

"You know what I think? I think you are scared of men in general. You seem to be that type."

She somehow knew he was trying to goad her, but she still felt the need to defend herself. "I'm not scared of men. What do you mean by *that type*?"

"The type who thinks being with a man is dirty or sinful. I think they call such people frigid or cold."

She felt insulted. "I grew up in the U.S. I dated plenty of men."

"Really? Romantic dates or play dates?"

"Romantic dates," she snapped.

He stared at her, until her bravado died and she began to fidget with discomfort. "Bullshit. I bet you would tremble and run screaming if a man tried to kiss you."

"Of course not. I-I've kissed plenty of times before and enjoyed it." She was lying, but she hated the way he was painting her as a pathetic loser who was scared of men or intimacy.

"Prove it."

"What?"

"You said you kissed plenty of times before and enjoyed it. So prove it."

"B-but..."

"You also said you didn't hate me. So kiss me and prove both those points."

"I-I..."

He raised an eyebrow, probably waiting for her to breakdown or back down. She didn't want to. She really did want to prove to him, she wasn't a silly frightened girl he imagined her to be.

Taking a deep breath, she moved closer to him, until there was barely any inches between them. His eyes continued to watch her, but he did not move.

Clumsily, her mouth brushed his chin and then the lower lip. She cringed, not only because she was trying to kiss a man whom she hated, but also because she knew she was a terrible kisser. She hadn't had enough practice, or rather, she barely had any practice.

But luckily and surprisingly, the effect of her kiss was a desired one. Abhay Singham didn't scorn or make fun of her kiss. He stiffened against her and went completely still. Barely a couple of seconds later, his long fingers held her chin in a firm grip.

He pulled her closer and pressed his lips to her's in a deep kiss—a burning hot and wet kiss that instantly heated her entire body. She felt stunned by her body's primal response even as she opened her mouth for his possessive invasion.

She might have started the kiss, but Abhay Singham took charge, and took it to a whole new level. He grabbed her hips with his large palms and with a few long steps pushed her on top of the bed. She gasped into his mouth at the impact as her back hit the mattress. Her body came alive as something sizzled deep inside her.

His lips met hers aggressively while he shoved her legs apart, letting her feel his erection on her core. Her body trembled with need for the first time instead of fear. Involuntarily, she began grinding against him to reduce the ache that started deep within her core.

He was a murderer, and he married her against her will. He kept her caged in his world, and yet her body came alive in his arms. He kissed her hard. and then pulled at her bottom lip, before moving to kiss her ear and her sensitive neck. His hands explored her now sensitive chest playing with her nipples as she came even more alive.

She began to moan and greedily explore him with her fingers. She traced his muscular chest, going over every impressive ridge that she recalled seeing during the mornings as he exercised.

Her fingers slowly slid down from his abs towards his hips, where she encountered something hard.

He froze.

"Fuck," he groaned into her mouth, and immediately one of his hands wrapped around her wrist, to stop her from exploring further.

"Bloody hell!" he cursed and rolled away from her.

She felt a keen loss and also disappointment as he got up from the bed. He was breathing heavily like her as he removed something from around his waist.

Slowly her muddled brain began to focus on the object he held in his hand.

A gun! He was removing the holster from around his hips and placing it on the nightstand.

He watched her now rapidly paling face and slowly a sneer formed on his. "What's the matter, my dear wife? Not that eager anymore after seeing one of my toys?" he taunted.

No sound emitted from her terrified brain.

He shrugged. "Just as well. I don't need your inexperienced kisses or moves. So you can go back to pretending you are asleep like always."

Anika felt hurt. No, not hurt—she was pissed off. She knew it was stupid to feel that way, considering he had a gun that was less than three feet away from him, and she was sure he knew how to use it very well.

But she rose up onto her knees. "Listen to me, Abhay Singham. You were the one who forced me into this marriage. You were the one who is forcing me to lie in your bed each night. And for your kind information, I'm not stupid. I felt your obvious arousal at my *inexperienced* kisses and moves. So save your big-bad-wolf and cocky attitude. And also, yes, I wanted something. I'm sick of not being able to do something significant with my time here. I want to set up a small clinic within the estate to be able to stock up medications and continue to help the people here. Knowing how you are a control freak, I need your help and permission first."

He froze at her outburst, and she saw his jaw clench, and she didn't know if it was in anger or frustration. She was betting more towards frustration as she could see his obvious and most likely an impressive arousal.

"This was definitely a mistake," he muttered under his breath and strode out of the bedroom, slamming the door shut.

*****

Anika stayed back in the room, feeling confused. Shaking her head off the weird thoughts that were taking up space in her mind, she spent some time on the computer, before going down to meet with the people.

Lakshmi smiled at her. "Abhay has asked all of us to help you set up a clinic in one of the rooms at the back."

Anika's heart leaped, and she felt her lips continue to tingle from the kiss. "That's good. Show me that place."

They spent the rest of the day cleaning the area, making it completely sterile. As they worked together, she overheard some conversation.

"That man deserved to be killed after what he did with our crop."

"Yes, he was apparently the same bastard who also messed with the fish pond, poisoning it. That's why Meena had a reaction a few weeks ago."

"What happened last night?" Anika could not contain her curiosity anymore. She was willing to risk receiving another threat from Abhay Singham.

"The Senani dogs that had set fire to the barn were finally hunted down."

"I'm glad Abhay killed those animals this time. They had set the barn on fire last year, too, and got away."

Anika winced at the casual manner people spoke regarding taking a life—the life of a human. Being a doctor, she found that completely unacceptable. She just could not understand how everyone, including the young impressionable minds in the area, accepted and justified the act of killing.

Unfortunately, she was bound to the man who was responsible for most of the killings.

Later that night, when he returned home early, surprisingly she didn't shrink away in fear. She kept eying him secretly as he prepared for bed.

"Oh my God, I'm so shallow!" she thought, when her eyes kept going to his lips and then his body as he took off his suit jacket.

She tossed and turned, willing herself to sleep, before he returned from the shower. Soon it was too late, as he came out in just pyjama bottoms, exposing his impressive chest. He was drying his wet hair with a towel and missed seeing her gawk.

Or so she thought.

"What is it now?" he asked, still continuing to dry his hair.

She jumped at being caught. "N-nothing. I just wanted to thank you... for the clinic."

He didn't reply. He threw the towel away on to a chair, and turned off the lights, before sliding into the bed, next to her.

She felt awareness thrum between them and felt confused. She still thought and knew he was a monster.

But the monster she was married to—was slowly growing on her.

CHAPTER TWENTY-ONE

"Lakshmi!" Anika called out, struggling to close the zipper on the back of her blouse. She stood waiting in the middle of the closet, feeling the weight of the embellished skirt. Lakshmi had disappeared a few minutes ago to borrow an eye shadow to match her skirt.

It was the day she and Abhay had to go to the temple as part of the Singham tradition.

I've been married for twenty-one days...

The thought should have terrified her and made her go into a nervous breakdown. If she hadn't been doing the things she did in the last three weeks, she would have definitely broken down in tears of misery.

Her thoughts were interrupted when her blouse threatened to slip down her chest. She wished she could have worn something else. It wasn't her plan to get decked up for the temple, but the entire household was extremely excited, especially Lakshmi. Anika couldn't say no.

"Lakshmiii..." She let out another call, and froze when she saw Abhay Singham entering the room. She wasn't expecting him to return so soon.

He watched her quietly for a long moment, until she was compelled to talk to break the tense silence.

"I-I uh needed help..." her voice trailed off not wanting to give him the details.

"Help with?" He seemed ready to go, wearing a traditional maroon turban and an ivory silk tunic. The attire made him appear even taller while giving him a majestic look.

Majestic? What is wrong with you?

Her thoughts confused her and she stood rooted to her spot, even as he walked towards her and stopped inches from her.

"Nothing. I-I don't need help. I'm good now," she took a step back to flatten her almost bare back to the wall.

His eyes traveled over her, and when they rested on the exposed skin of her midriff, she held her breath. She didn't move and was very thankful when Lakshmi returned..

"Sorry, I forgot about your blouse." Lakshmi stepped into the bedroom with a smile and froze when she saw Abhay Singham.

He didn't turn to look at Lakshmi. His eyes continued to explore Anika lazily. "Close the doors on your way out," he instructed softly.

"Yes. Yes. Of course. Sorry," Lakshmi murmured and was gone in a flash.

"What do you need help with?" he asked with a hooded look.

"I don't need help, I'm fine."

He continued staring, making her extremely aware of his presence. She held her breath and controlled the urge to squirm.

"Are you ready to go?" he asked.

"I just need to do a few more things. I'll be done in ten minutes." The back of her blouse was open, and she crossed one hand over her chest to keep the blouse from falling off her shoulders again, and revealing a good portion of the upper part of her breasts.

Something flickered in his eyes and he slowly stepped closer.

Her heart began to thud wildly. Was it fear, or anticipation, or both, she didn't know.

He was less than a couple of feet away from her, but he didn't stop. He continued to walk closer. "Remember, you are supposed to convince people that this marriage has been consummated. Can you do it?" His voice was hypnotic.

"Yes." Her voice came out in a whisper.

He stopped in front of her, and placed his arms on either side of her on the wall, caging her in. She raised her head and kept her eyes locked to his as her breathing turned uneven.

Her body jolted in surprise when she felt his fingertips graze the skin on her midriff.

"You need to stop fidgeting every time I touch you." His breath threatened to burn her skin, and his fingertips left a trail of goosebumps. She also felt her nipples pebble as an involuntary response.

"I'll be fine," she said with a slight tremble in her voice.

"You are jumpy right now. That's not very convincing." He spoke in a deep, seductive tone.

She wanted to say something, but her voice got caught in her throat when he pulled her off the wall, and turned her to push her against it. Before she could process anything, she felt him tug on the stuck zipper on the back of her blouse, ultimately parting it completely.

She remained frozen, trying not to show any reaction. There was nothing supporting the blouse now. All he had to do was to push it off her shoulders, and she would be left completely naked from above the waist.

She waited with bated breath, for what she didn't know.

"The zip was stuck," his warm, moist breath murmured in her ear.

Then she felt a hot and wet trail, left behind by his tongue on her ear. His tongue swirled, teasing her skin, tantalizing her entirely.

She bit down on her lower lip to suppress a moan that was threatening to escape. Her breathing got heavier as he continued tracing the tip of his tongue down to the nape of her neck.

Remember, he's a monster!

But you know why he does some of these things...

Are you crazy? He forced you to marry him!

She clenched her teeth, refusing to give in, although all she wanted to do was turn around to pull his lips to hers. She gathered up all the willpower she could muster, not to give in to her natural urges. But still her breath came out in a hiss as he nuzzled the sensitive skin on the back of her neck, and then continued lower on her bare back.

"Abhay..." His name rolled off her lips for the first time as she addressed him directly. "We're running late to the temple," she managed to say in a steady tone.

His lips froze, and then slowly he let go of her waist. He pulled the ends of the blouse together and zipped it smoothly before stepping away from her. She felt a keen loss of his warm touch. Her knees had turned to mush, but she turned and looked at him.

His eyes were blazing hot and he ran his eyes over her.

"Fifteen minutes," he stated curtly, before striding out of the bedroom.

Ten minutes later, she sat next to him in the back seat of his SUV on their way to the temple. She felt the awareness and lingering sexual tension within the car.

She looked out of the window, trying to ignore his presence, remembering the last time she had been in the car with him. At that time, she had wanted to jump out of the running car to escape, but stayed put, only for her family's safety.

However, at the moment, his proximity stirred something within her, something she wasn't prepared for. She felt confused. A part of her mind was trying to rationalize the violence. Everyone had said that in order to protect what was rightfully theirs, they had to resort to violence. In the civilized world, violence was never justified even if it was to protect.

This is not the usual civilized world. People make and follow their own laws. So maybe it is justified.

She shook her head to get rid of such thoughts. She couldn't help but notice that the entire household, and seemingly the entire region, respected him and treated his wish as their command. He was more or less their ruler.

But what made an educated man like him turn into a brutal ruler?

"How is the setup of the clinic going on?" he asked, making her jump at his sudden voice.

She turned towards him, expecting him to be annoyed by her jumpiness. But he had an impassive look on his face.

She cleared her throat that seemed to always get stuck in his presence.

"I need more medications. I also need access to a computer with a video set-up so I can get the people treated by doctors online. Doctors with specializations."

He watched her closely as though to check her sincerity in wanting to help his people. He knew that his people hated Prajapatis and also the other way around.

"I'll have a computer ordered for the clinic," he said. Then there was a glint. "You want me to order one for your personal use too? Or are you happy breaking into mine each day?" he asked.

She was stunned because she had made sure he had not seen her using his computer.

"I--I was getting bored and I needed something to do." She was embarrassed, and it didn't help that his eyes continued to watch her in mild amusement.

"You can use mine. But it would be easier if you had your own computer."

"Thank you."

There was more silence, making her hyperaware of him.

Her cheeks heated as she recalled the feel of his lips and hot breath on her bare back, an hour ago.

A part of her, had desperately wanted her to turn at that time, to know how those soft but firm lips would feel on her bare midriff, and also to know how they would feel as they moved higher.

She rubbed her arms conspicuously to get rid of the goosebumps that appeared on her skin. She had to make an effort to sit still and not gravitate towards him within the car.

She sighed internally in relief when they reached a visibly crowded temple.

CHAPTER TWENTY-TWO

Anika spent the next couple of hours performing several rituals during the ceremony. She felt a lot of eyes on her.

The Singhams were probably assessing if she was a worthy bride. Strangely, instead of being offended, she was more understanding of their attitude.

Abhay sat next to her but they didn't talk to each other. They followed the instructions of the head priest. Each time, their hands brushed, or he touched her lightly as a part of some ritual or the other, she felt a zing pass through her, reminding her of the moments they had spent before leaving for the temple.

"Please stand up and take the blessings of the gods," the priest instructed, concluding the ceremony.

She wasn't a religious person but her mother was. Since her childhood, her mother made it a point to take Myra and her to the temple every month. More than the actual praying, she enjoyed the aura and the peacefulness she found there.

She missed her mom and sister. Even though she had not lived in her childhood home since she was eighteen, they had always been close and spoke regularly.

People at the temple began to clear out. She waited quietly as Abhay spoke to some people. She noticed how they took in his words and instructions without any arguments. She knew they trusted him. They trusted him not only with their lives, but also with their family's lives. Being a doctor herself, she understood how much strain that kind of responsibility would add on a person.

Abhay finished talking and began to head back. When he saw her waiting at the entrance of the temple, a surprised look passed on his face.

"Ready?" he asked.

"Yes."

He held her elbow and led them to the car. She slid into the backseat, next to Abhay and stared out of the window.

"What's wrong?" he asked as though sensing her mood.

"Nothing," she replied. "Just missing my parents and sister."

There was silence.

"They can visit you anytime. Just let me know a few days before so there is adequate security."

Shocked by his offer, she stared at him. "Thank you," she whispered.

He gave a nod before going back to checking something on his phone.

A few minutes later, they drove into what appeared to be a hospital. There were parked ambulances in front of the building.

The car stopped by the main entrance with a flight of marble steps.

"Come." She heard Abhay's soft command and watched him as he got out of the car. Curious, she followed him.

They passed through the security guards, and the polished corridors as Abhay walked with purpose towards the back of the building. He stopped in front of a room and opened the lock. It was storage of some kind, filled with boxes.

"I couldn't find anyone to set up a proper pharmacy within the hospital," he said, looking at her with a closed-off expression. "Pick up whatever you need from here. If there is something else, make a list, and I'll have someone bring it to you."

She nodded. Over the next few minutes, she picked out a few items of everything she needed to help the people with their minor illnesses.

"I'm done," she said, after filling an empty box with what she needed.

He was waiting silently, seemingly angry and upset about something. She knew that was his usual state of mind, but something about the way he stood, scanning the boxes, made her think there was more frustration involved.

"Was this a running hospital before?" she asked.

He was quiet, and then looking at her hands while she held a large box filled with medications, he answered her, "Yes. It was one of the best until a couple of decades ago."

"What happened?" she asked softly.

"The feud started," he replied. "None of the doctors or nurses wanted to stay where their families could be in danger."

The way he said it, made her aware of his frustration and helplessness. It was strange, but she felt the need to comfort him.

He was the reason; her aunt was controlling her life. He could also be the possible reason for her to remain captive at this place for an unforeseeable future, but at that point, she somehow empathized with the man in front of her.

He wanted to end the violence. He wanted to see his people prosper. He spent days and most of his nights, trying to protect what was his from others who were bent upon destroying all the work he did for his people.

She took a deep breath tamping down the words that were trying to burst out of her mouth—about wanting to know more about him. "I have everything I need for now."

Abhay nodded curtly and took the box from her hands. While they headed towards their car, Anika noticed that the hospital was still maintained well. There were no visible cobwebs or mold anywhere inside. She guessed there must have been people dedicated to cleaning and maintaining the place, in the hope it would thrive once again.

She stopped as her attention fell on a large painting of a familiar woman hanging about the exit doors.

"Was that your mother?" she asked. The image was of a simple, pretty woman with a bright, kind smile.

Abhay's posture became rigid. "Yes, that was my mother," he replied, stopping in front of her with his back facing her to look at the picture.

The picture filled her with sadness. She knew that Arundhati Singham was adored and revered by each and everyone within the Singham Estate. She had heard so many tales about that woman she felt as though she knew her.

"She was beautiful... inside and out," she said softly.

She heard him take a deep breath. She wasn't sure if he was angry because he had warned her not to talk about his mother, or whether he was caught off balance by her statement.

"Yes. She was very beautiful," he said quietly, his tone not giving anything away.

She was slowly beginning to understand more of this man who was her husband. She knew he was hurt and even sad remembering his mother, but he didn't lash out at her like she had expected him to.

"Let's go, it's getting dark," he said, continuing towards their car.

She sat next to him and briefly looked at him. His face was unreadable as always, and he simply stared ahead as the car moved.

The mixed feelings she had towards Abhay confused her. On one hand she knew she would somehow and eventually save her family from harm, but on the other hand she wasn't as excited as she thought she would be to go back to her old life in San Francisco.

Instead, she wanted to know more about the man who was her husband. Even though the circumstances in which they came together were less than ideal, she felt the need to explore more.

Was it just passion?

CHAPTER TWENTY-THREE

Anika's life fell into a pattern over the next week as she spent more time in the clinic. She continued to spend time on the computer during the day between her clinic appointments. During the evenings, after spending time at the library, she retired to the master bedroom.

She no longer pretended to be asleep in the mornings. In fact, she waited up for him to have dinner together. Apart from some minor conversation she made regarding the people and their medical needs, dinner was mostly silent.

They didn't say a lot to each other, but something was building up between them, and each time he was next to her on the bed, she was intensely aware of his presence. Her body hummed when they accidentally touched, and whenever he got up in the morning and went away, she keenly felt his absence. Their suite felt empty and cold when he wasn't around.

There were times when she was honestly afraid of him, especially when he came back with blood on his clothes. It still bothered her a lot, but when he showered and slid in next to her, she forgot everything.

He didn't make any move to touch her again. The last time he did was before they had gone to the temple.

She tried to convince herself that she wasn't disappointed. She should be happy that she knew he wouldn't touch her anymore.

But the disappointed hollowness in her stomach spoke the truth.

*****

Anika was having breakfast outside at the gardens. She was laughing at something Sonu and Meena were saying.

"You girls don't have to go to school today?" she asked.

"No. It's the beginning of our summer holidays!" Sonu said excitedly.

Lakshmi was rolling her eyes. "That means these little imps are going to attack the mango farm. The last time they ate so many mangoes, they suffered stomach aches for a few days."

Meena grinned. "Pfft... it was nothing. We got back on the trees the day after, and we felt fine."

Anika smiled. "Well, I have the medications handy this time. Just don't forget to bring me some of those mangoes."

"Definitely! I know which trees have the juiciest and sweetest ones, but please don't tell Abhay about us going to the orchard."

Anika was amused. "Why? He'll ask you girls to bring him back some as well?"

Sonu grinned. "No. He'll give us a talk about how it's not safe climbing trees and all. I fell from a tree three years ago and broke my leg."

Before Anika could say anything, she heard someone shout.

"Dr. Singham! Sitamma just collapsed! Please come quickly."

Leaving the half-eaten breakfast, Anika rushed towards the prone woman. The woman's face was graying, and she was clutching her chest.

"Keep her upright! She might be having a heart attack." Anika turned towards Malini. "Please have a car readied. We cannot treat this at the clinic. I'll have to go to the hospital."

Malini nodded and left hurriedly. Meantime, Anika asked a few people to get a stretcher to take the patient to the car.

As soon as they reached the parking lot, Malini returned with a tense look. "We are trying to reach Abhay, but we are not able to connect with his phone."

Anika frowned. "Why is that relevant right now? Have the car readied, and we can reach him later to let him know."

Malini looked uncomfortable. "Anika, we all have strict instructions to contact him before we can take you anywhere outside the estate premises."

Anika's jaw hardened. "Well, that may be the case under normal circumstances, but this is an emergency." She turned towards one of the men. "Get the car here. We are going to the Arundhati Hospital. That's my order."

Her heart beat faster as she spoke to them with a firm tone. She knew the people here were accustomed to authority, and right then, she needed to enforce it to save a life.

The man only hesitated for a couple of seconds before he went towards a car.

Twenty minutes later, they reached the Arundhati Hospital. Dr. Rao was also waiting for her. A few hours after they administered proper medication and took necessary precautions, Sitamma seemed to stabilize.

"She still needs proper monitoring. We need to take her to the city," said Anika.

Dr. Rao nodded. "I can go along with her and also take someone."

"I can come along—"

"No. You can't," said another voice.

Abhay Singham stood at the hospital room doorway with a face like thunder.

Anika looked at Dr. Rao. "Please leave right now Dr. Rao and let me know how she is doing after reaching the city."

Dr. Rao nodded and left with the patient, but before he walked out of the room, he threw her a concerned look.

Abhay began walking towards her slowly. "You disobeyed my order."

Listening to the quiet statement, Anika felt a shiver run through her body.

"I didn't disobey on purpose. We had an emer—"

"You even made my people disobey me."

"They didn't disobey you, Abhay," she reasoned. "They were following my instructions."

Instead of cooling him down, her statement made him even angrier. "You do not *ever* override my instructions." He emphasized the word ever.

"But it was an emergen—"

Before she could finish, he closed the distance between them completely. "Do you understand?" he demanded with a scary quiet tone.

"I had to make a quick decision because—"

"Do you understand?" he snapped.

Anika was pissed. She was a doctor. She was trained to save lives, not compromise someone's life because of a blind order.

"No!" she shouted.

His expression changed. He became even more menacing. And he also seemed to grow in size as he loomed on top of her.

"What did you just say?" he asked quietly.

"I said no!" When he continued to loom, she shoved him hard on his chest with both her hands. "I will not follow your orders blindly! I did what I had to do!"

He didn't budge with her shoves. In fact, his eyes blazed. He looked downright scary, but she refused to get intimidated by him.

"I don't care what the circumstances are. I want you to follow my orders. I will not tolerate any disobedience—"

"I don't care either," she snapped, getting angry herself. How dare he behave as though she was a child who had to obey his order blindly? She was a qualified doctor who will be required to make many such calls in the future.

Before she could give him a piece of her mind, the next instant, her legs were lifted off the ground, as he pinned her to the wall with his body. She gasped at the impact, and soon she was facing her enraged husband as he held her hips in a firm grip.

"Don't fucking test my limits," he hissed into her face.

She glared at him. "Then don't put any limits on me!" she snapped.

There was silence. Then she heard his teeth grinding. "It is for your bloody safety," he said with anger.

She felt some of her anger die at his words. "Then why didn't you tell me that instead of barking out instructions at me?" she asked softly.

He glared. "Because I don't have to explain myself every time. When I pass an order, I expect people to follow it."

Okay, she was back to being pissed at him. "I'm not other people, I'm your wife! If you want me to follow something, you explain it to me first so I can make an informed decision."

He continued glaring at her in frustration.

Slowly, she felt her anger die completely. He was worried about her. In his weird way, he was trying to keep her safe from being attacked by his enemies.

She understood him to an extent, but she did not want to let him think he could order her around without providing a proper reason. Although she had been behaving like a doormat initially due to the circumstances, she wasn't one. She needed to set the tone of their relationship, however brief it would be.

Her feet were still off the ground. Slowly, she wrapped them around his hips, pulling him closer. He stiffened at the contact, and she felt him hardening.

She moved her hands from his shoulder to his head, and tugged his hair. Leaning forward, she kissed him on his cheek. "I'm sorry I worried you," she whispered.

His hands on her hips tightened. She waited breathlessly, wondering whether he would push away from her or pull her close to take over the sexual tension threatening to blaze between them.

Before anything happened, a man's voice interrupted them. "Abhay, they are waiting for you. We should start now. Oh! I didn't know. I mean I'll... uh... I'll be outside."

They heard the man leave.

Slowly, Abhay let her loose until her legs slid down, and she stood on the ground in front of him.

He watched her closely. "I'll make sure to leave behind more men at the estate from now on. They'll accompany you if you need to go somewhere," he said quietly.

Anika nodded. "Thank you," she replied and then watched him adjust his clothes. "Are you going home?" she asked huskily.

Regret flashed in his eyes. "No. I had to cut short an important meeting. I'll be heading back to the city. I'll be back tomorrow morning."

"Okay. I'll see you at home tomorrow," she said softly.

He nodded and then held her elbow and walked them towards waiting cars.

As her car drove away, she turned back and saw him standing next to his car watching her.

When she couldn't see him anymore, she sat back with her eyes closed and rested her head against the seat.

She had referred to the Singham Estate as her home...

CHAPTER TWENTY-FOUR

The next day, Anika was at the clinic jotting down the list of supplies before setting them up. She was checking for the side effects of one of the medicines when she heard her name called.

It was Abhay. He was back home early, and for some reason he sounded angry.

Heart pounding loudly, she started running out of the clinic towards him. A week ago, she would have probably run the other way at his bellowing of her name, but she somehow knew he wouldn't hurt her. As the voice came closer, she heard the urgency in his tone along with anger.

Her feet stumbled and slowed down when she saw him.

Abhay was carrying an unconscious girl in his arms. She realized it was Sonu because Meena was walking next to him barely able to stand on her own feet.

"Oh my God. What happened?" Anika asked as she rushed towards them. "Get her inside the clinic. Lakshmi, bring in hot water and the first-aid kit."

Meantime, Abhay placed Sonu on a bed that she pointed to. "Lakshmi, help clean up Meena while I check Sonu," she instructed.

Her hands shook as she checked Sonu's pulse. There was dried blood on the girl's lip and several bruises all over her face and neck. She somehow suspected there might also be at other places.

Who could do this to a child?

She began cleaning the surface wounds and applied antiseptic to the bite marks.

"Is she going to be okay?" Abhay asked.

"I think so," she said based on Sonu's pulse.

"Go get me that bastard," Abhay told someone. She heard the shuffling of several footsteps as the men left.

Meena was lying on a bed next to Sonu. Even though she was conscious, she lay very still staring blankly up at the ceiling in shock while Lakshmi cleaned her wounds.

"What happened, Abhay?" Anika asked as she continued cleaning the bite marks and scratches on Sonu.

"They were taken by the Senanis, and by the time someone heard and found them, they were already tortured."

Anika sucked in her breath. "Abhay, can you wait outside? I want to check whether they have been... touched." She couldn't use the word rape when it came to these innocent girls. She had grown so fond of them and their innocent jokes.

She saw the rage in Abhay's eyes as he felt equally tormented at the thought of the girls being violated in that way.

"I'll be in the courtyard," he said before walking away.

Anika checked Sonu first. She felt immense relief when she found the proof of her innocence. She stood next to Meena who was still staring blankly up at the ceiling.

"Meena," she said, placing a gentle hand on her. "You are okay now. You are back home and safe."

Silent tears rolled out of Meena's eyes as she continued staring at the ceiling.

"Are you in too much pain, Meena?" Anika asked gently. "Let me know, so I can give you something to help."

Meena broke into soft sobs. "I feel so dirty," she said.

Anika's heart clenched. She held Meena's hand and squeezed in reassurance. "They took us from the mango orchard," Meena said between silent sobs. "Sonu and I go there often during the season. We were in a tree, plucking a few mangoes and eating them, when we saw the two men waiting below and smiling at us. We tried to escape, but they grabbed us. They kept laughing and touching us when we fought back and started to scream for help. One of the men was about to do something bad to me, but he was stopped by the other man. That man said virgins would get a higher price when they sold us and that there were other ways to have fun. So he..."

Anika clenched her fists as she heard the details of the abuse the child had to suffer at the hands of those animals.

"You are okay now, Meena. You have been so brave. I am proud of you." Anika gave her a pain medication along with a mild sedative that would help relax her.

Anika stayed by the girls, allowing only a few people to check on them. The whole household was tense and outraged.

A few hours later, both the girls gained consciousness and were able to talk a little. Anika had warned the people not to ask the girls about the attack.

When it was almost dark, and she had just finished having a small meal with the girls, she heard shouts.

A few minutes later, the door to the clinic crashed open.

Gasping out loud, Anika stood up. Abhay was covered in blood and standing at the clinic doorway.

"Abhay..." Anika froze at the rage she saw in his eyes.

"Sonu, Meena, come with me," he said quietly.

Anika went towards him and stood at the doorway. "Abhay, the girls are resting."

"They can rest better after they see this." His voice held a grim purpose, scaring her.

"Abhay... please. They are just children."

"Anika, get out of my way." The look in his eyes made her want to step aside, but she didn't budge from the doorway.

His eyes flared at her resistance. She thought he would shove her aside and grab the girls, but he looked behind her. "Let's go," he said softly.

To Anika's utter shock, Sonu and Meena were standing right behind her with a determined look on their faces.

Anika stepped aside allowing them to go. She felt helpless, but she couldn't stop them from going if they wanted to.

They walked towards an open courtyard where two men were tied to a pole.

"Were these the men who touched you?" Abhay asked the girls in dead calm.

Sonu started crying. "Yes! He hurt me!" She pointed to one of the men.

The men were badly beaten and were bleeding profusely.

"Hurt him, Sonu," Abhay instructed gently.

To Anika's utter shock, Sonu wiped away her tears and went towards the man. Someone handed her a long metal rod. She took it into her hands and swung at him.

There were sick thudding noises and screams as the rod met with the tied man's flesh.

When Sonu got tired and was panting while watching the man with satisfaction in her eyes, Abhay looked at Meena.

"Meena, your turn," he said simply.

Meena didn't wait. She moved towards the other man in fast strides. She took another rod and began hitting hard. Sonu joined in on the beating.

Over the next few minutes, the sick thudding noises continued until both the girls stopped and panted. The men were slumped against the poles. *Were they dead?*

Abhay strode to the men and checked their pulses. "Wake them up," he instructed in a chilling tone.

A couple of women brought in containers filled with water and splashed the water against the tied-up men, but the men remained unconscious.

"Anika, wake these bastards up."

She jumped as she heard Abhay speak to her.

"What?"

"Wake them up. We are not done with them. Everyone needs to be made aware of what happens when they touch innocent girls."

Anika felt torn.

"Wake him up, Dr. Singham," Sonu pleaded.

Anika was stunned by the heartfelt request from Sonu. The tied man had violated her in the worst way possible. Even though he had not raped her in the technical sense, the fact he stole her innocence was equally bad. She closed her eyes, took a deep breath and opened them again. "Lakshmi, please bring my medical bag."

Ten minutes later, Anika gave both the men adrenaline shots.

The men slowly gained consciousness. After being splashed by more water, they began to beg for forgiveness.

"Please, don't. I'm sorry. I won't come into the Singham lands again. It was a mistake. I won't touch another Singham girl." One of the men cried and pleaded, wetting himself.

"Please," the other man begged. "It was a mistake. I thought she wanted it. In fact... she... goaded me... she even called me there and—" He stopped when he saw the rage on Abhay's face.

"After tonight, you both won't touch any girl, let alone a Singham one," he promised.

He picked up a long leather whip and hit them. The whip sliced into the men's flesh, flaying it open. Screams filled up the air again. Soon, there was silence. Both the men were slumped against the poles.

Abhay didn't ask Anika to wake them up again. And seeing the pallor on the men's faces, she knew the adrenaline shots wouldn't work on them anymore. They were gone, and strangely, the fact didn't bother her.

When Abhay threw the whip on the ground and stepped away from the men, Sonu and Meena ran towards him and hugged him from both sides. "Thank you, Abhay," said Sonu as she cried softly.

"The animals that hurt you both are dead," he said softly. "You don't have to worry anymore. Just make sure you take someone with you whenever you are going far from the estate."

The girls nodded.

Later that night, Anika checked on the girls one more time before going up to the bedroom.

Abhay hadn't returned yet. She knew he might have been instructing his men to clean up the bodies and blood from the courtyard.

She had taken a shower and was freshening up in the bathroom when she heard the door to their suite open and then the bathroom door.

He was still in his bloodied clothes. But unlike last time, she wasn't scared and didn't feel hate for him.

She went closer to him.

He was trying to unbutton his shirt but his fingers were stiff from the dirt and blood on his hands.

"Let me help," she said softly.

He stood still, and didn't say anything while she slowly opened each button on his bloodied shirt. She pushed the ends apart and away from his broad shoulders. She couldn't completely remove it due to his height, so he helped by shrugging out of his shirt.

Meantime, she tugged open the button on the waistband of his trousers. He froze when he felt her fingers, but didn't say anything.

She looked at him quietly for a few moments, before walking towards the sink to wash the blood off her hands.

She saw his reflection from the mirror above the sink as he stepped out of his clothes completely and walked towards the shower.

He was completely naked as he washed the blood away. Unlike last time when they were in a similar situation when she was in the tub and he in the shower, she could now see his entire body and not just a partial view. Her eyes took in every ridge over his muscular body as he moved.

And also unlike last time, she was not terrified. In fact, she craved him at that moment. She wondered what he would do if she opened the door to the shower stall and joined him.

Taking a deep breath before she gave in to her crazy impulses, she dried her hands and walked out of the bedroom.

A few minutes later, Abhay joined her on the bed as he lay next to her. He was staring at the ceiling lost in thoughts.

Slowly and tentatively, she moved closer to him and placed her arm on his bare chest.

He stiffened at the touch, but slowly his body relaxed. He didn't say anything.

She curled her arm properly around his waist and fell into a deep comforting sleep.

*****

Sometime during the early hours of the morning, she stirred awake. She turned her head and felt a keen disappointment when she didn't find Abhay lying next to her.

She sat up slowly and saw him slipping a gun into the holster around his waist. He was completely dressed.

He lifted his eyes towards her as though he felt her gaze. Slowly, he came towards the bed and stood next to her.

He cupped her face with one hand and began to lower his head watching her the entire time, as though waiting to see whether she would pull back at some point, but she didn't.

Her heart thudded in anticipation as she waited for his kiss. As soon as his lips met hers, she sank into it completely. She closed her eyes and met his tongue as he kissed her deeply, but before she could touch him and pull him closer, he pulled away.

"I have to go now. I have people waiting for me downstairs," he said gently.

She felt disappointed, but she nodded.

"I'll be gone for a week to sort an issue with permissions for one of our manufacturing units. Will you be okay?" he asked.

She nodded again. "Yes," she said, even as she felt the loss of presence already.

He watched her face for a few more moments before turning back and leaving their suite.

Anika fell back on the pillows to go back to sleep, but she couldn't. She slowly touched her lips with a finger still feeling the tingles from the kiss.

CHAPTER TWENTY-FIVE

"As of now, we have all the approvals to begin the work starting next week." A well-dressed man sat opposite to Abhay and Dev in the boardroom of their company headquarters.

"That's good, Tiwari. You can discuss the details with Dev. He will be managing the new units as well."

Tiwari nodded. "Thanks, Abhay," he said and then picked up the folder in front of him before leaving the room.

As soon as the door shut with a soft click, Dev groaned. "Three more units? Are you trying to kill me? With what I have now, I barely get to visit home with all this work."

"These units are critical for our people. They are the primary source of proper employment."

Dev frowned. "I know that. But what I don't understand is why the fuck we can't have other qualified people take care of these manufacturing units aside from me? You know I want to be home more often and take care of the problems there."

Abhay didn't respond. He watched Dev as he got up from the chair to go towards the area where some of the drinks were kept.

He knew he was working Dev pretty hard, but he had no other choice. Dev was a hothead, and he was bloodthirsty when it came to dealing with the feud. Whenever he was home and tackled with some of the issues, it always ended in bloody carnage.

It wasn't like Abhay didn't shed blood or kill. But he only did it when he absolutely had to—not for the pleasure of it.

"What are the Senanis up to now?" Dev asked, pouring scotch into two crystal glasses.

"The usual," Abhay replied, not offering any details.

"Why are we putting up with their crap? It'll take us one sweeping attack to take them down," Dev remarked, and Abhay knew there was some truth to it in the short term. The short-term solution was not his goal—he wanted to regain peace to the region so it would last forever.

Dev continued when Abhay did not respond, "You know we have a hundred percent chance of taking them down with Ravi and rest of the men back." One of Abhay's key players and bodyguard had parted from the Singham's when he found out about the alliance with the Prajapatis. They returned after they had heard about what Anika was doing and also after the barn incident.

"We just need to take one of the Senani brothers. Hemant Senani must go."

"Dev, don't forget they are our relatives."

"Bullshit, they don't care. Look what they did to the barn," Dev retorted.

"The man who did it is dead. The day I find out the brothers have also been involved directly in our business, I will deal with them."

"That's more like it."

"Did you attend the Randheep Trust Fund meeting?"

"Yes." Dev took a shot from one of the glasses. "The profits are up again. If Randheep was alive, he'd be one rich kid." He poured some more amber liquid into the glass and shot it down again.

It was barely five in the evening.

Abhay saw the shadows in Dev's eyes when he spoke of Randheep. He knew that even though Dev was only seven when it happened, the past still haunted him and affected him very strongly.

"Is everything okay with our other neighbors? Or is the bitch and her goons still wreaking havoc within our lands?" Dev asked with a sneer, twirling his glass in agitation.

"Dev."

"What? I just wanted to know. I should have killed her when I had the chance. Now, unfortunately you are married to her cousin."

"We are in peaceful terms with the Prajapatis. I don't want you involved in anything without checking with me first."

"Okay, fine." Dev took another shot. "Enough about the devil, let's talk about your angel instead. So tell me big bro, how is married life treating you?"

Abhay sat back in the chair, watching the city view outside their high-rise building. "As expected," he replied calmly.

Dev laughed. "Really? Is that why you were hurrying the talks this past week? Because you want to get back to your boring predictable marriage?"

Abhay didn't respond, but that didn't deter Dev. "Oh, come on. People at the Singham Estate are waiting with bated breath for several little baby Abhay Singhams to run around the mansion halls. Although personally, I'd rather have pretty little nieces who look like Anika."

Abhay didn't comment. Before Dev could say anything, they were interrupted by a knock. "Dev, Miss Tia Mathur is here to see you."

Dev groaned. He placed the glass on the counter and stood up straight. "Tell her I'll be there in a few minutes."

As soon as Dev's assistant left, Abhay frowned. "You are drunk tonight. Are you driving?"

"I'm not drunk," said Dev with a mock offended look. "And besides the lovely Miss Mathur is going to be driving." He shrugged on an evening jacket that was lying on one of the chairs. "Heard she might win the best actress award tonight. If she does, then we'd be celebrating until late. Don't wait up for me." He winked and grinned.

A week ago, it had been a tennis star. Before that, a socialite. Each month there was a different woman.

Abhay watched as his brother brushed his hair back with his fingers and popped in a piece of chewing gum.

"I don't care how late you are out, but I expect you to be there at the site tomorrow morning by eight."

Dev groaned. "Eight! It's a freaking Sunday tomorrow for god's sake."

"Eight sharp, Dev." His tone implied no arguments.

"Fine," Dev grumbled, and left the room.

Getting up from the chair, Abhay poured himself a drink.

He took a big sip and closing his eyes, he let himself feel the searing trail of fire burn from his throat to his stomach. The slow burn within reminded him of his wife—the wife he hadn't even wanted in the first place.

Anika Prajapati was one of his sacrifices. Even though he had hated the very idea of marrying her because of their family's history, he still went ahead because of a long-held promise.

When he had married her, he was sure he would loathe her. He had even braced himself to a hate-filled marriage that would bind him for an eternity.

However, his wife turned out to be an enigma. She was terrified of him and hated him. Yet, right from the beginning, she spent her days helping his people even though she didn't really have to. At first, he had felt suspicious, but observing her over the past few weeks, he realized she was being genuine.

She wasn't even close to being the woman he had imagined. When Neelambari Prajapati had sent him the proposal of marrying her older niece, he was not surprised. The only thing he knew at that point was that she lived somewhere abroad. Neelambari had spoken to him and told him about how her niece fantasized about marrying someone who was handsome, rich, and influential such as him. He knew it wasn't just his ego that made him believe her. At that point, he had already met a lot of women who had similar aspirations and had wanted to become Mrs. Abhay Singham.

But the only difference with Anika was that she had the Prajapati blood to qualify as his potential bride. The only other woman who had that qualification was Sabitha Prajapati, but he knew that even considering Sabitha as a potential bride would make Dev go on a rampage.

That ultimately led to Anika Prajapati being his bride.

He knew as soon as Anika saw the violence in front of the temple, she must have realized the harsh realities of marrying a man such as him. She had wanted to back away.

At that time, he was barely managing to maintain peace between the Prajapatis and Singhams, and he knew that if she backed out on the marriage, it would end in bloodshed. He had been pissed and angry that she would even try to do so when she gave her word. She had no choice, but to be his wife. They were bound by a promise that would tie them together until death because he did not believe in divorce.

He had tried to give her more time, ignoring her initially, but it only left him frustrated and aching. He did not believe in cheating. And because of that, he recalled how each night he had to jerk off in the shower imagining his wife's face and body before laying next to her on their bed. He hadn't trusted himself not to roll over and take her like he craved whether she was willing or not.

Slowly and steadily, she was getting under his skin. He was becoming obsessed about wanting to see her smile or just watch her as she slept. He even enjoyed their little talks when she spoke about her day and his people. Sometimes she pushed him hard, challenging his authority. Instead of pissing him off, it only made him crave her more.

He recalled how she had looked and felt when he kissed her before leaving for the city. That particular scene ran in his mind over the last four nights, leaving him even more restless. He distinctly recalled how she had arched towards him and wanted his touch. She had looked disappointed when he had told her he was leaving.

She's mine, and she wants me.

With that thought, a fire restarted inside his body, and this time it threatened to turn into an inferno.

He made a call on his phone. "Bhalla, get the car ready. We are going home tonight."

"But, Abhay. You are supposed to meet the ministers for dinner at nine."

"Make the necessary calls and cancel it. I want to be home tonight."

Abhay ended the call as his heart beat faster in anticipation.

He was going to claim his wife tonight.

CHAPTER TWENTY-SIX

It had been four days since Abhay had gone on a trip, and Anika was missing him badly. She couldn't escape the fact she was falling for Abhay Singham.

It wasn't because she was married to him, and she was expected to live with him until death, but because she had started to like and respect him as a person. Everything he did for his people and the lengths he went to bring justice, truly moved her. There was also the fact she found him hot, extremely hot.

The arrogant, masculine face, the chiseled muscles and his tall, strong body, which had once been a cause for her fear... were part of her dirty fantasies. She wanted to touch him badly. She wanted to explore him inside and out until she knew everything that was Abhay Singham.

"Uhhh...Anika?" a woman's voice interrupted her daydreaming.

She blinked her eyes slowly and saw Lakshmi's amused look. "Yes?"

"I have been asking you whether you wanted to have dinner in your suite or at the dining table tonight, but you just kept staring through me with a silly smile on your face."

Anika blushed. "Umm... sorry about that," she replied with a sheepish smile. "I think I'll just shower and go to bed tonight. I'm not that hungry after having so many treats this evening."

Lakshmi smiled. "People are pretty grateful for your help here, and want to repay you in the form of homemade treats, but you don't have to indulge everyone. I'll let them know they should stop providing you so many treats."

"No. That's okay. I really enjoyed the treats." Anika was touched by the people's gesture. Most of them had a long hard day of work either in the fields or around the estate, but they took the time to make her special dishes to show her their appreciation.

"There are other reasons, too," said Lakshmi, with a twinkle in her eyes. "Some of the people think you are already carrying the Singham heir and want to fatten you up."

Anika blushed once again. "Oh...I... uh am not. Pregnant, I mean."

Lakshmi burst out laughing shaking her head in amusement. "Anyway, I'll bring up some buttermilk and fruits. You can have them if you are hungry later on."

Anika thanked Lakshmi before calling it a day and headed up to the master suite.

After a long, relaxing shower, she was sorting through her clothes in a large ornate drawer looking for a nightdress. She realized it was high time she needed to hang her clothes in one of the large walk-in closets in the suite.

She had just found one of her comfortable cotton nightdresses when she heard the soft click of the master bedroom door.

Immediately, she felt the change in the atmosphere of the room. Without even turning, she knew it wasn't Lakshmi with her meal, and that it was *him*.

Abhay Singham had returned. Her towel-clad body quivered as she felt the heat of his stare on her back.

She heard the soft footsteps approach her, but she refused to turn towards him. Her breathing began to grow heavy as a strange tension gripped her body. Her nails dug into the intricate carving of the dresser as she felt him close the distance between them, until he stood right behind her.

His body emitted heat that slowly enveloped her, making her belly quiver in awareness and need. She waited for him to touch her, but he didn't, and that somehow made her even hotter. She clenched her legs together and tried to regulate her breathing.

"Turn around," he ordered softly, his warm breath behind her ears causing her to shiver once again.

Slowly, she turned around keeping her eyes downcast. She felt his eyes on her towel -clad body, and then she felt his fingers trailing around the edges of the fabric leaving goosebumps in their path. His warm lips trailed the path laid by his fingertips. She closed her eyes as tremors ran through her body and let out a soft involuntary moan. Her knuckles turned white as she held onto the dresser behind her to support her weakening legs.

His lips slowly moved higher towards her neck and then behind her ear. "Spread your legs," he rasped.

Trembling, she did as he ordered. She was a virgin, and although she knew the technical aspects of sex, she had no experience with something like this. But she knew that whatever would happen between them tonight would be something she would enjoy immensely.

Sucking in her lower lip and keeping her eyes closed, she waited for him to make the next move.

"Do you want my touch tonight?" His tone contained an edge to it.

Moaning softly again, she nodded and arched her back inviting him to touch.

She gasped as she felt his huge palms cup her breasts through the soft towel.

He began massaging them. "Tell me how much you want this," he said, his tongue running over her earlobe and ending with a stinging bite. The pleasure pain of the bite caused another set of tremors to bolt from her breasts to her womb.

"I want this," she whispered.

Slowly, like she was a gift, he loosened the knot and let the towel fall from around her.

Despite the cool air on her exposed body, she felt so hot, she could barely breathe through the intense pleasure she felt.

"Open your eyes." His fingers caressed her bare breasts and then slid lower to her belly and then around her hips. It almost felt like he was familiarizing himself with her shape.

Shuddering, she opened her eyes to look at him. She could only see the top of his head as he was kneeling down running his large palms over her spread thighs continuing his exploration. Something primitive ran through her body as she looked at the dark head of the powerful, dominating man kneeling in front of her for the sole purpose of pleasuring her.

She jumped when one of his long fingers brushed against her sensitive folds. Her breath came out in loud pants. She felt extremely embarrassed, but also highly aroused at the same time.

"Shh... we'll go slow," his voice came out as a deep rumble next to her core causing it to quiver. His eyes met hers, trapping her in some sort of trance due to their intensity. "I just want you to enjoy my touch."

She nodded her head.

"I know you are scared of me and maybe even hate me, but I'll make you feel good until you crave my touch."

"I do," she exhaled noisily. "I do crave your touch."

As soon as the words escaped her, a feral, possessive smile appeared on his face, and the next instant, she felt his mouth closing in over her core.

She gasped out and clutched his hair. Her legs threatened to give out, and the only thing holding her upright—were his arms wrapped around her hips, pinning her back to the dresser.

She felt his tongue explore her, building some kind of tension and pressure inside. She moaned and continued fisting his hair, tugging him even closer. Her entire body hummed, and she tried to move her hips frantically. She tried to move closer to him, but his strong arms kept her trapped in place, and his mouth continued to wreak havoc inside her body.

Her body writhed to his touch, and she felt the pressure inside increase until it became unbearable. She shuddered unable to handle the build-up and finally let go. She came with a low keening sound, her body trembling violently as she felt the waves of intense pleasure crash through her body.

Slowly, she regained her awareness. She was panting, and she felt his hands run over her stomach and hips in a soothing manner as if to calm her down. He waited for her to completely calm down before sweeping her off her feet without another word.

He carried her out of the closet to the bed and placed her on it and lay next to her, his body seemingly tensed. When he didn't make any move to touch her again or demand anything in return, she turned towards him. His eyes were closed shut.

"Abhay?"

"Yes?" he gritted out.

"Can I... touch you?" Her eyes ran over the silk fabric of his shirt, tempted to open the buttons and explore him the way she had wanted to for the past few days.

His eyes opened and met hers with an intensity that began to build a slow fire inside. "Yes, touch me any way you want."

He looked tired with shadows under his eyes. "I... uh... won't disturb your sleep?" she asked.

A small smile broke on his harsh face. "I can hardly sleep when my wife is sitting naked next to me watching me with that hungry look."

Her cheeks heated, but she slowly placed a hand over his shirt feeling the crisp hairs underneath. She wanted to give in to her desires, but the fact that he was watching her made her feel shy. In the end, her curiosity and need won.

She slid her hand underneath the shirt and pressed her palm to the warm flesh. Abhay groaned and shifted his hips. She saw that his trousers had risen due to his erection, and felt an immediate thrill that her simple touch could do that to him.

Her hand grew bolder, and she began to open the buttons on his shirt revealing inch by inch of beautiful, chiseled, golden skin, and muscles. She trailed her fingers along the line of hair that disappeared into the waistband of his trousers.

She bit her lip as she hesitated. *How far can I go?*

The next moment, Abhay eliminated the dilemma by rapidly unbuttoning his trousers and pushing them down his legs. He placed his hands on either side of his head, an indication to her that he was hers to explore.

His breathing had quickened, and his eyes continued to watch her with a hooded look. Feeling bold, she slid her hand on top of his underwear stroking his arousal through the fabric. Another deep groan vibrated through his body.

Slowly, she pushed down the elastic of his underwear revealing a portion of his manhood. It was thick and larger than she had imagined.

"Abhay... can I kiss you there?"

"Do anything you want with me," he rasped.

She held him and squeezed him with her fist fascinated by the smooth texture of the rock-hard organ.

He emitted a hiss making her quickly let go of him. "Don't you like it?" she asked.

"I love it," his voice was thick. His eyes glittered in the relative darkness as he watched her intently.

A strong need began to rise in her. She wanted to drive her husband crazy until he lost control because of her. She leaned down and pressed a small kiss on the velvety skin.

His hips bucked, and his body shook. "I want to take your... you into my mouth." She didn't want to use a clinical term.

His hands crept to her hair. "Call it a cock, Anika. Say that word for me," he growled out the order.

"Cock," she said softly. "I want to take your cock into my mouth, and give you the same kind of pleasure you gave me."

His eyes closed, and he groaned out in pleasure. "Fuck! I love hearing those words from your pretty mouth." Tightening her hand around his cock, she bent down to take the head into her lips and sucked it into her mouth.

His breath hissed. "Don't use your teeth."

She let go immediately. "Oh! I'm so sorry, I never did this before."

She felt foolish. Over the years, out of curiosity, she had watched a few videos where a woman pleasured a man with her mouth, but she didn't realize until that moment that there was more to it than simply taking it in and sucking.

"It's okay," Abhay reassured, the back of his hands running along her breasts and waist making her shiver. "Go on…"

Opening her mouth wider, she took him in again, this time letting his cock rest on her tongue. She looked up to see if he liked it this time.

"Fuck!" he groaned, pushing her long hair away from her face so he could see her mouth clearly. "You are so fucking beautiful."

Feeling encouraged, she continued to pleasure him slowly moving him in and out of her mouth. His hands stayed on top of her head, guiding her, letting her know she was doing it right.

Both their breaths came out in loud pants, and soon his body began to shudder violently. She understood he was close and quickened her movements, until suddenly he pushed her away.

He moved on top her and held her breasts with both hands pushing them together as his cock jerked over her belly, letting out warm spurts of his need for her. His eyes closed as he continued to come, until slowly his body lost the tension after the release.

She held her breath when his eyes opened locking her in his gaze. Then, without another word, he leaned down and kissed her, his tongue moving inside her mouth possessively, making her moan as tension began to grip her body.

She realized how embarrassingly aroused she was once again, as his fingers moved downward and slid inside her wet core. She continued moaning as his head slid down and explored her neck and then her breasts with his lips. His mouth made wet noises as he sucked and acquainted himself to her sensitive breasts. He nipped her skin until the sharp, pleasurable pain on her nipples along with the pressure from his fingers on her sensitive clit made her explode in a series of shudders.

She didn't know how long her orgasm lasted, but when she gained awareness, she felt boneless and satisfied. Her eyes met his as he continued stroking her gently.

"Wait here," he said before getting out of the bed and disappearing into the bathroom. He returned with a wet, warm washcloth and used it to wipe away the traces of him on her body.

"I can clean myself..." She stopped midway and let him continue when she saw the feral look on his face.

She supposed she should feel embarrassed or ashamed, because what they did over the last few hours was so dirty and wicked, but all she felt was excitement.

After cleaning her up, he disappeared into the bathroom again where she heard the shower running. Minutes later, he returned and slid naked into the bed next to her. He pulled her close until she was half lying on top of him.

Her body felt relaxed, and she curled against him as exhaustion took over, and she slid into a deep content sleep.

CHAPTER TWENTY-SEVEN

It had been a week since Abhay had come home and drastically changed their relationship dynamics. It was the most exciting time of her life, and she never expected to be where she was. She was constantly smiling like a fool thinking about all the naughty things they did together without going all the way. She wanted to be with him all the time—she wanted to be part of his every waking moment to talk to him and listen to him.

It was an unspoken pact they would enjoy each other until they feel the need to consummate their marriage. She liked the fact they were taking it slow. After he showed her the ways a man and woman could please each other, she had become an addict. She felt like a teenager wanting to explore her sexuality.

They could not keep their hands off each other, but they had their own set of priorities. The only time they had common goals was when Abhay returned home each night until the morning.

Anika stirred when she heard the alarm go off. Slowly, she fluttered her eyes open when she heard a groan rumbling under her.

She was sprawled naked over her husband with her cheek against his chest. Tightening her hold on him, she took in his musky scent that was a combination of expensive cologne and their passion from last night.

She stretched like a cat when Abhay's large hand started to move over her bare butt in smooth strokes indicating his wakefulness.

"Let's stay in longer this morning," she purred, burrowing into his neck.

Abhay chuckled.

"Please," she begged.

"No excuses," he rumbled out.

"But it's chilly outside, and this feels so good." She tightened her hold on him.

He was quiet, while he continued to stroke her back.

"Why do we have to go each and every morning?" She burrowed even deeper as she hugged him.

At her slightly whiny tone, there was another amused chuckle.

She raised her head to look at him. Slowly, she smiled, putting on what she termed inside her head as her sultry expression. "You know what we can do if we stay in?" she asked, rubbing her lower body over his morning arousal.

She saw his heated look and smiled. "Imagine doing that until it's time for the clinic to open."

His hands tightened on her hips and pulled her closer, making them both groan in pleasure. But the words that came from his mouth were completely contrary. "It's five fifteen, Dr. Singham. We need to be out in another fifteen minutes, so either hurry up and get ready, or I'll drag you as you are."

Anika glared at him before rolling away. "Dominating, controlling, infuriating, taskmaster," she grumbled as she stood shivering next to the bed.

She saw an amused smile on his face, and she smiled back as she began to get ready.

Ten minutes later, they rode towards the range.

Anika was standing with her legs slightly apart, with one eye closed and the other focused on her target.

"Shoot!" At Abhay's instruction, she pulled the trigger, and there was a loud noise.

This time she only recoiled back slightly. During her first practice, she fell on her ass, and it smarted for a couple of days.

"Not too bad," he said as he watched the target.

Anika grinned. "You mean, at least it hit the target's knees even though you were asking me to aim for the head?"

Abhay had a flash of amusement in his eyes before snapping back to his serious taskmaster mode. "All right, I need you to stay focused on the target. This time, I'm going to give you a smaller gun. Ten more rounds and we can be done for the day."

Anika groaned internally as she continued to follow his instructions. After the attack on Sonu and Meena, Abhay was taking additional precautions when it came to the security of the people living within the Singham lands.

He wanted everyone to carry a weapon and since most of them learned how to shoot a gun as children, his focus fell on Anika. As soon he had returned from his trip, the next morning he had dragged her to the shooting range, before even the sun rose, to teach her how to defend herself.

During their private moments, Abhay was hot and sexy while being playful on rare occasions. But when it came to her security, and things like—her learning how to shoot—he was dead serious. He pushed her again and again, until she met his expectations.

"That's much better," he said, when she hit the target in the middle.

"Do I get a prize?" she asked.

"Ask me anything, and I'll have it delivered in no time."

She laughed. "No. Not that kind of prize. The prize I want is to be able to spend an entire day with you."

He watched her while he contemplated. "Done. How about tomorrow? I'll push my appointments."

Anika was excited. "Really? I'll check whether Dr. Rao can handle the appointments I have."

Thirty minutes later as they stepped out of the shower and were getting ready for their day, she asked him. "Can we go on some kind of picnic within the estate grounds?"

"The orchard," he said. "You'll enjoy it there, but it might require us to take additional security along."

"Oh." She felt disappointed. She was hoping for a more private place. "I think spending our time within the house is fine."

He watched her and then contemplated something before he answered. "There is another place that is relatively more private and also secure. The Singham Lakehouse. Let's go there."

*****

"You are pregnant," Anika announced to a visibly shocked woman.

The woman had come to the clinic with the complaint that she could have possibly been suffering from food poisoning.

"You are a goddess, and you definitely being here is a blessing, and will lift the curse. I never thought I would be a mother. I have been trying to conceive for the past ten years with no luck."

Anika smiled at the woman. "I haven't done anything except for announcing the news."

"I can't wait to tell my husband. I'm sure he will want to thank you personally." The woman beamed.

"That's not necessary, and I am also close to wrapping up here. You are my last patient for the day."

"I will ask Ravi to come by when he gets back. He went with Abhay today," the woman stated.

Anika realized the woman was the wife of one of Abhay's trusted men who had returned after the incident at the barn. Ravi was her bodyguard appointed by Abhay after her hospital debacle. "Congrats again to you and Ravi."

The setup of the clinic was getting bigger and bigger day by day. Anika had the important equipment like the ultrasound machine moved to the clinic from the hospital.

Dr. Rao also offered to expand his hours to look after the patients. Abhay was still actively working on hiring more doctors so that the Arundhati hospital will once again be a working hospital. Meanwhile, Anika had suggested he hire a few more doctors who were willing to offer video consultation.

After seeing the woman out, she went to the kitchen and spoke with the cooks about packing some ingredients for the picnic the next day.

"Where are you and Abhay going?" Malini asked, looking visibly excited.

Anika smiled. "To the Singham Lakehouse," she answered.

There was a sudden shift in the atmosphere. Everyone froze visibly.

"Abhay is taking you to the Singham Lakehouse?" Malini asked.

This time, Anika didn't smile. "Yes. What's wrong?"

There were few more moments of silence before everyone burst into cheers and began clapping and jumping excitedly.

"What? Tell me what is it?" Anika asked.

Most of them exchanged glances eager and wanting to tell her.

"We can't. We are not allowed to talk about the family. Ask Abhay," said one of the women.

Anika didn't push the women to tell her. She knew that even though Abhay was softening towards her, he was not the kind to allow anyone within his household to break an explicit rule. "Okay, I'll ask him tomorrow," she said, smiling at them.

That evening, she spent some more time at the library working on the computer and also going through a few books. She was interrupted when Abhay scooped her up from the sofa at the library to carry her into their room where their dinner was waiting.

CHAPTER TWENTY-EIGHT

The next morning, Anika stepped out of the main door where a convoy of six cars was waiting. One of the men held the door open for Anika as she slid into the passenger seat next to Abhay.

They drove for almost an hour before finally arriving at the gates of what appeared to be a huge orchard.

"We will be here all day. Have a perimeter drawn," Abhay instructed to his men before leading her towards the clearing within the trees.

As they walked through the clearing, Anika could hear the gentle flow of running water.

"Is there a river?" she asked with visible excitement.

Abhay smiled. "A lake," he said.

Ten minutes later, she gasped at the sight in front of her. A huge lake was hidden past the trees, and it was surrounded by wildflowers of vivid colors. A small cabin invitingly stood to one side. "It's breathtaking!"

He led them closer to the cabin and pushed the door open standing to one side to let her in. She gasped once again, taking in the sight that was simple yet beautiful. One side of the cabin was made completely of glass with a view to the lake.

She turned to look at him. "It's so beautiful. Thank you for bringing me here," she said softly.

He dropped the picnic basket on the small intimate dining table before he pulled her closer and kissed her. She moaned, feeling lost in the moment—completely overwhelmed by the man in front of her, and by the beauty surrounding them.

Minutes later, they pulled away to gasp for some much needed air. She placed a hand on his chest stopping him from picking her up. She laughed, "Wait! I have a special treat for you. Let's have breakfast before you sweep me off my feet," she teased.

He didn't let go of her waist, but he didn't sweep her into his arms either. Laughing again, she moved towards the picnic basket and brought out the neatly packed silver dishes.

Everything at the Singham Mansion was larger than life. Lakshmi was horrified when Anika asked her for some plastic containers and bottles to carry the food for the picnic. She insisted everything be packed in crystal and silver containers.

Abhay pulled a chair out for her while she set some of the containers and bottles on the table top along with two plates. She served a generous portion onto his plate and put the remaining onto hers. By the time she finished serving, he sat opposite to her.

"Your feast awaits, my Lord," she said, smiling at him.

"My Lord?" he asked in amusement.

"Yes. I'm pretty sure this is the first time I'm ever using expensive china plates, crystal goblets, and silver dishes for a picnic!"

He laughed softly, while picking up a shiny silver fork and knife. As soon as he took a bite of the breakfast wrap and chewed, he froze.

"How is it? I made it this morning. Do you like it?" she asked with an anxious look on her face. She had woken up early to help in the kitchen for preparing the dishes she wanted to take for their day out.

His face held a somber look, but he nodded. "I love it," he said.

Anika bit into the wrap that contained spicy shrimp, eggs, and walnuts. It tasted awesome, but the heat in the dish made her reach out for the chocolate milk she had poured into the crystal glasses.

Abhay took a sip from his glass as well and froze again.

He placed the fork and knife on his plate to watch her with an expressionless look. "How did you find out?" he asked quietly.

Anika didn't pretend not to know what he was talking about. She had thought to surprise him and maybe even make him happy when she decided to put together this special meal, but the look on his face made her doubt her decision.

"How, Anika?" he asked again. "My mother was the only one who knew I liked the combination of shrimp and walnuts. Even if that turned out to be a guess from your side, the fact that I also like the unusual combination of chocolate milk with salt crystals is something you could not have possibly guessed."

Anika bit her lip. "I found a book of her recipes in the library," she said. "Some of them had your name written on top."

He was quiet. "I see."

"Are you... angry?" she asked tentatively.

"No," he answered. "I was just reminded of her."

Anika let out a sigh of relief inside.

"Thank you for putting this together," he said, watching her with a look that both melted her heart and also made her want to do dirty things to him right then.

She took a deep breath to control herself. She realized that even though they had become physically close over the last couple of weeks, beyond talking about their day in general, they had never spoken about any personal stuff.

She watched him as he ate and felt her face heat up.

"What are you thinking?" he asked, continuing to watch her with heated gaze.

"I just realized that we know each other so intimately... well, at least in the physical sense... I mean, not completely physical... but..." She let out a short laugh. "You know what I mean," she finished.

There was amusement in his eyes. "Hmm. I guess what you are trying to say is that each night you let me kiss every inch of your delectable body. But the fact that you don't know much about me, apart from how I taste and feel, is bothering you. Am I right?" he asked.

"Yes," she squeaked out, taking a long sip of ice-cold chocolate milk to cool her down.

He smiled. "Ask me whatever you want," he offered.

Ever since she was brought into the Singham land as his bride, there was just one burning question in her mind. "Why did you marry me, Abhay?"

At her question, he paused for a few seconds before looking at her with an impassive look. "Because I made a promise to my grandmother."

She was stunned. For some reason she did not think of him as someone who listened to his grandmother when it came to picking his bride. "What promise?" she asked.

"To marry a Prajapati."

Anika's heart began to thud. "But I heard from my aunt that it was to break the curse. I thought you married me because the people of the lands wanted it. What has it got to do with a promise to your grandmother?"

"I don't believe in curses, Anika," he replied, further shocking her. "Yes, I do care for my people, and I respect the traditions of my ancestors within reason. And according to the tradition, I was supposed to marry a Senani woman, but my grandmother wanted me to marry a Prajapati instead."

"Why?"

"Because when it was my father's turn to marry a Prajapati, he decided to break the long-held tradition and marry for love."

Anika frowned. "What's wrong with marrying for love?" she asked.

"Nothing, except for the fact that when you are born in families like ours, and a land like ours, a part of your life belongs to the people and the long-held traditions."

Abhay said ours as though he considered her to be a part of the land. "But I don't really belong to your land. I grew up living in a different continent altogether."

"I know," he said quietly. "But your aunt sent a proposal saying you were enamored by what you had heard about the Singhams. That you had a long-held fantasy of marrying someone rich and powerful from your father's land."

She frowned. "I never said those things."

"Yes. I guessed that a few weeks ago," he said dryly.

"So you thought I wanted to marry you willingly, and then changed my mind?"

"Yes."

"But you saw I was terrified of you in the beginning."

A flash of regret passed on his face. "I believed your aunt. It didn't strike me that she might have fooled you in any way. Believe me, that wasn't the first time I had received wedding proposals from women living in the Western world. They thought it was romantic and exciting to live as a rich and powerful wife in a dangerous part of world."

Anika believed him. She knew there were women who fantasized about marrying sheikhs or mobsters or dangerous powerful men. "I don't find marrying a stranger the least bit romantic."

"I know that now. But during the wedding, I had thought you developed cold feet *after* seeing the violence in reality, in front of the temple, where we were supposed to meet for the first time. By then, there was too much at stake to back out of the wedding."

Yet another reason to hate her aunt. She had lied to Abhay about her being a willing bride.

"What kind of stake?" she asked instead wanting to know desperately.

He was quiet.

"Please," she insisted. "I need to know why I was brought here under false pretenses. I want to know why no one is allowed to speak about the Singham, Prajapati, or Senani families."

"For your protection," he answered. "Before our wedding, I warned everyone not to speak about our families because Singhams hate the Prajapatis. They have been killing each other for as long as thirty years. Whenever someone spoke about the feud, it always enraged people and ended in some violence. That's why I passed a strict rule that no one should ever speak about the families and the past."

"I still don't get it." She frowned. "If Singhams and Prajapatis were enemies because your father didn't marry according to the tradition, why would Senanis be enraged and destroy our lands and try to hurt our people?"

He smiled.

"What?" she asked wondering why he was smiling at a serious question like that.

"You said our lands and our people." He observed.

Anika was stunned. He was right. She didn't know when, but slowly she was becoming used to the place and its people.

She shook her head. "So tell me, why the Senanis enraged?" she asked once again, then immediately she frowned. "Because you broke the tradition of marrying a Senani. They feel insulted."

He nodded when she guessed correctly.

"But why did your grandmother risk offending the Senanis for the sake of making amends with Prajapatis?" she asked.

He sighed. "It's a long story, Anika. I know you want to get all the answers, but all I can say is that my grandmother took a risk by assuming that Senanis would understand her decision, and she would be able to compensate for the hurt ego and disrespect shown to your aunt."

"Why would the Senanis understand your grandmother's decision?" she asked.

"Because my grandmother was a Senani."

Anika had a wiggling doubt deep inside. "What was your grandmother's name?"

"Devasena Singham."

Holy Mother of God! Anika had been reading Abhay's grandmother's journals.

She bit her lip deciding whether or not to reveal that she had been snooping around his library. Taking a chance, she told him. "I found your grandmother's journals. I've been reading some of them in the library."

There was surprise in his eyes, but he didn't get angry. "Yes, my grandmother was an avid reader and wrote for pleasure. I have some of her journals within our suite as well."

"Yes, that's how I found out about them in the first place. Your grandmother was a fiery woman with a kind heart."

"Yes, she was." There was a fond look on Abhay's face.

"What happened to Abhimanyu Singham?" she asked.

"Anika..."

"Please. I need to know," she pleaded.

Abhay sighed. "He was killed by your father's brother."

Anika was stunned and sad. "What? Why?"

"Because the Prajapatis were enraged about the fact that my grandfather didn't do anything to stop my father from marrying my mother. So they pretended to be guests who had come to congratulate the newly married couple and attacked my grandfather instead."

Anika sucked in a breath. "They killed your grandfather at your parents' wedding?"

"Yes."

"Then what did the Singhams do?"

"My immediate family didn't do anything, but some of our relatives attacked your grandfather and killed his wife by accident. She apparently took the shot meant for him. They also tried to kill your grandfather after, but he survived, only to be completely paralyzed."

"Oh my God," she whispered.

"Let's not talk about that, Anika." He pushed his chair back and got up.

He came towards her and pulled her up from her chair before carrying her to the bedroom.

He placed her gently on a soft mattress and began kissing her. He slowly pulled up her top and threw it aside, kissing her neck and moving downward.

She moaned softly as shivers ran through her. But though she was aroused, her mind kept revolving around what they had spoken about a while ago. Abhay must have sensed her distraction, because his mouth paused, and he slowly sat up.

"I'm sorry," she whispered. "It's just that I have been here for nearly three months now, and I became used to you and our people. But I won't be able to be at peace without finding out more about what led to our marriage."

He sat back, leaning on the bed and sighed. "What do you want to know?"

"How could Devasena, I mean your grandmother, be okay for you to marry someone who belongs to the family who killed her husband?" she asked.

"Like I said before, when you grow up like her, part of your life belongs to the people. She wanted to end the bloodshed. She was so strong and relentless that she wanted to do right by the Prajapatis even though..."

It was unlike him to hesitate at saying anything. "Even though?"

"Even though the Prajapatis ended up killing both my grandmother's sons and also my mother and youngest brother."

Anika was stunned. "How?"

"After ten years of my parents' marriage, your father and his brother invited my family to the temple on the pretext of discussing a wedding proposal between your aunt and my uncle. But instead, your uncle attacked and killed my mother leading to mass bloodshed that eventually killed your father and uncle, too."

Her heart thudded. "I was told my father died in a fire accident. My mother believes the same, too."

Tears filled up her eyes, as she thought about how she lost her father to a senseless violence. "I can't believe this." She looked at him through blurred eyes and felt her heart clench. "How can you even bear to be with someone whose family is directly responsible for the death of your parents and brother?" she asked.

"It happened a long time ago, Anika."

"No wonder the people hated me and mistrusted me when I came here."

He ran a gentle hand on her back. "They treat you like their goddess now. You have helped them so much, and they can see that you genuinely care."

She wiped her tears away to look at him clearly. "What about you?" she asked. "You must have hated me at some point."

He was quiet. "Yes," he answered. "I resented the fact I was forced to marry the daughter of a man who was my father's best friend and who betrayed him in the worst way possible." He looked at her, and she flinched at what she saw. "There were times when I wanted to make you suffer for your father's sins."

She closed her eyes unable to look at him. "How old were you when..."

"I was nine, and Dev was seven, and my little brother was only five. Dev and I stayed home with our grandmother, and my parents took my other brother along."

"I'm sorry," she whispered.

"Dev and I were told it was an accident when it happened, and our grandmother kept us away from this for the longest time. She put us both in a boarding school in London. Until I got a call with the news that my grandmother had suffered from a long terminal illness, I had no idea about the feud or what had happened to my parents. Even my grandmother didn't tell me much at that time. She only made me promise that I would marry a Prajapati woman."

Anika could imagine Devasena being so selfless. Even when she knew she was dying, she was trying to protect her grandsons. "Why did you not go back after your grandmother died?"

"I could not. People were dying, and the ones living were about to die because of the draught, and they were convinced it was a curse. The curse of a woman who was betrayed. All I was interested in was to build peace and make our lands prosper once again at any cost."

Tears filled up her eyes once again. "I am so proud of you. I don't think anyone would have chosen the life you did given the options you had." She recalled seeing alumni magazines of Oxford University where he must have graduated.

He wiped away her tears. "I never for a minute regret any of the choices I made," he said.

She held his face. "I don't want to either," she said. And then she kissed him softly on his lips. "Make me a Singham bride for real. I want to be yours in every way."

Abhay's eyes flared at her declaration. He kissed her while she desperately pulled away at his clothes.

"I want you," she whispered when he pulled away to trail his lips down her neck licking and nipping on the skin.

"Take me now, Abhay," she pleaded.

As if those were the magic words he needed to hear, he growled, pulling away from her to remove his clothes. He pulled away the remaining clothes from her body, and threw them on the floor next to his. He went back to her, his body hot and aroused just the way she wanted him.

His fingers touched her breasts, then slowly slid down her stomach and finally went between her quivering thighs. He spread them and cupped her core. Slowly, a long finger entered deep into her while his thumb rubbed her clit.

She gasped in pleasurable pain. Over the weeks, he had gotten her used to his body and had given her immense pleasure, but never had he entered this deep within her core. His finger went in and out of her, creating a friction and making her needier.

She clenched against his finger each time he rubbed a spot that made her thrum with desire for him. Her body felt electrified as she felt an intense buildup starting within.

"No!" She shook her head vigorously, trying to push his hand away from her.

She opened her eyes to see his tense face. "I want you inside me when I come. I want to come with you," she demanded.

He watched her face for a second before kissing her hard. He then looked down towards the place where their bodies would soon join together.

Holding himself with one hand, he began guiding himself to her entrance. They both watched and groaned as he rubbed the tip up and down her slit before slowly sliding in.

As soon as he entered her, she gasped and closed her eyes. It was painful.

He stilled completely on top of her. When she opened her eyes, she saw him watching her closely.

"Breathe," he told her gently as he held her in the most intimate embrace. "The pain will fade soon, and all you'll feel is pleasure," he promised.

He began to slowly thrust in and out causing her to dig in her nails into his back as pleasure and pain warred inside her.

He leaned his face much closer to her and licked away the tear that had slid down her cheek. At the tender gesture coming from a ruthless man who led a hard life, her heart filled completely. She knew he was meant for her. He was the missing piece that had caused her to ache with emptiness before, the void that compelled her to know more about her roots.

He filled her mind and body moving faster, stronger, and deeper within. She met his moves with her own learning the rhythm that joined them together.

It still hurt, but it hurt in the most pleasurable way possible. She closed her eyes becoming lost in the intense feeling. She felt his tongue as it slid between her lips moving in and out with the same sensual dance.

Faintly, she heard a distant rumble from somewhere. She ignored everything but the man who possessed her. She twisted and writhed underneath him as she began to feel the familiar sensation of losing control. She began to clench around him as she thrashed and bucked harder underneath him. He held her down firmly letting her orgasm crash through her in waves.

"You are beautiful when you come," he rasped.

She continued to come harder, screaming his name, and feeling consumed by him.

He began to move inside her once again, pumping harder, losing control himself. She watched him through her haze as he let go thrusting into her deeper. She felt him grow larger inside her before he let out a roar and called out her name.

Their breaths came out in loud pants as he slumped and rested his forehead on hers.

A few moments later, he rolled away and pulled her into his arms.

When she finally calmed down, her nose prickled with a distinctive smell, and she saw the drops cover the large windowpanes of the bedroom.

It was raining.

CHAPTER TWENTY-NINE

"It's raining!" Anika sat up shocked as she heard and watched the heavy drops falling on the windowpanes.

"I know," he said, pulling her back to bed to lie next to him.

"But how can it rain? There is supposed to be a draught for the past thirty years."

He smiled. "Yes, but sometimes there are these small showers once in a while. Not a whole lot to help with the crops or fill up the water table with drinking water, though."

She frowned slightly. "I see."

They held each other as they watched the rain.

"Tell me about your family," he asked, moving his fingers lazily on her back, drawing patterns.

She couldn't control the automatic stiffening of her body, and his fingers stopped caressing.

"What's wrong?" he asked.

Anika didn't know what to tell him. On the one hand, she was tempted to tell him everything about how she was brought to India under false pretenses and then blackmailed into marrying him. But knowing her aunt, she didn't want her aunt to find out and fly into a rage and order the killing of all her family members.

She decided to tell him the truth when she got her parents and Myra to safety. In the meantime, she tried to get her body to relax and enjoy the moment with him.

"Nothing. I was just missing my parents and sister."

His fingers resumed their caressing. "I told you that you can invite them over anytime."

She sighed. "I know. I spoke to them. They said they'd visit soon."

"Good. Now tell me about your family," he asked again.

"I have a mom, stepdad, and a half-sister named, Myra."

"I already know, Anika. I want to know more…"

"Wait. You know about them?" she asked, her heart thudding.

"About them, yes. Before I married you, Dev had a file prepared with yours and your family's information in it."

"I know," she said.

"You know?"

"Yes. I overheard you and Dev talking on our wedding night. You were telling him that if I didn't listen to your orders, you'd arrange an accident and marry a Senani next."

There was a rumble underneath her ear as Abhay's chest shook with silent laughter.

"What is so funny?" she demanded.

He shook her head. "Apparently not the joke I was making at that time."

"A joke?"

"Yes, a joke. I can joke, too, Anika," he said dryly.

She shook her head chuckling with self-depreciation. "I can't believe that it was a joke I heard. I was terrified of you that night and the nights that followed, worried you would kill me for real if I didn't listen and follow your each and every order."

"And I was just disgusted with the whole situation. You kept shaking like a leaf each time I was around," he said. He tugged her hair back until she met his dark intense eyes. "Whenever I saw you, I was torn between wanting to truly behave like a savage animal you thought I was because then I would have an excuse to possess you the way I wanted to. You were so beautiful that each and every night when you slept next to me, it was torture."

"And now?" she whispered.

"And now... I'm addicted. I'm so addicted to you I don't think I can be without having your taste on my tongue or your sexy smell part of my every breath."

Anika's eyes widened as she heard the almost poetic way Abhay had expressed about how he felt about her.

"I'm addicted to you, too," she confessed. And then, slowly she moved on top of him. "Maybe we should both cure our addictions together," she said as she slowly kissed his chest and then moved down his body.

He groaned and held her hair as she pulled him into her mouth. She pleasured him the way he had taught her over the last few weeks.

"I want you in me again," she told him huskily.

"You'll be sore. I might hurt you."

She had a determined look. "I don't care. Just take me," she ordered.

With a growl, he flipped her on her back, and then he slowly returned the favor. His mouth met her intimate folds, until she was dripping wet again and thrashed about restlessly. Only then did he slide back into her.

It burned, but she welcomed it. She felt each and every inch of him inside her, filling her again and again, joining them together. She never wanted it to end.

He bent his head down to pull her nipple into his mouth. He sucked the tight bud, until she screamed.

He moved to the other bud and repeated, and this time she was begging him to take her hard. And so he did. He thrust hard—hard enough to shake their antique headboard and repeatedly bang it against the wall.

She screamed his name, and pulled him closer, shouting for him to make her his completely.

And so, he did. When he came, he shouted, "You are mine!"

*****

They fed each other lunch, during which she told him about her parents and Myra.

"My mother married my stepdad when I was seven, almost a year after I thought I lost my dad in an accident in India."

"I see."

"No, it's not like how it sounds. She wasn't actually looking to marry someone. It just happened, I guess. My stepdad was a colleague who worked at the same hospital as her. He told me he had fallen in love with her the moment he met her, but my mother married my father who swept her off her feet. When my father died, and she went into pieces, my stepdad helped us mourn and move forward."

"You are close to them," he said. He stated that rather than asked.

"Yes. Very close. Even though we sometimes got on each other's nerves, not a day went without speaking to one another."

He frowned. "Have you spoken to them after coming here?"

She only hesitated for a couple of seconds. "Yes, a couple of times," she lied. "I told them about the invite and they are excited to visit us."

He was quiet.

"My parents are on a cruise until the next month, and Myra... she'll have a college break in a month too. Maybe they can visit us then."

His face relaxed.

"What about your friends?" he asked. "Do you have a lot of them back in San Francisco?"

131

"No. Not a lot. Just a few I made during college and one good childhood friend." She told him about Nathan.

"Why didn't you have more friends during childhood?"

She shrugged. "I had a stuttering problem until I was almost twelve. Kids made fun of me, and most of them didn't want to be associated with me. Nathan was the only one who was willing to overlook it and became a good friend."

Abhay looked angry.

She smiled, then reaching her hand, she wiped away the frown lines from his face. "Hey, it was a long time ago. Kids can be cruel sometimes. But I'm glad that whatever friends I made were the kind to stick with me through thick or thin."

He nodded.

They got up from the table and went back to the bedroom. He sat with his back against the headboard and pulled her closer, wrapping his arms around her waist, until she leaned back against him. They could see the lake from the bedroom window.

She asked him about how it felt growing up away from his grandmother who was one of the only surviving blood-relative.

"It was hard," he confessed. "Each time I came home for the holidays, I saw how my grandmother had to deal with so many things by herself. The feud had become even worse. Not only did my grandmother have to try and maintain peace, but she also had to ensure the people in the province had a good source of livelihood."

Anika's awe with Devasena grew even more. "She must have had an iron will."

"Yes, she did. Not once, even when I was old enough to help, did she ask me to do so. She told me to finish my studies and even wait until Dev finished his before we returned."

"Was it hard?" she asked softly. "When you returned under different circumstances?"

He was quiet.

"Yes," he replied, after a while. "My grandmother had known for a while that she was dying. But she kept it from us until the last moment. I was quite angry, confused and worried at that time."

Anika gently squeezed his hands around her waist in reassurance.

"My grandmother passed away three months after we had returned for good. She had told me several times that she had a lot of confidence in me about being able to run the Singham Estate and to take care of the people within. But I wasn't quite sure."

Anika's heart went out to him as she thought about how he must have been grieving, but at the same time he had to deal with such huge responsibility.

"How did people react to you taking over?" she asked.

"Not good," he replied with a self-depreciating laugh. "I increased the profits of the manufacturing units, planted drought resistant crops, and did everything I could to keep the people from starving. But it took me close to two years to prove that I was capable of leading them effectively. And that was only after I shot down a group of violent Prajapatis who had attacked us."

She listened as he told her how he had wanted to avoid violence at first, but then when the Prajapatis were repeatedly taking advantage of the fact, he had to ultimately resort to violence.

"What about Dev? How did he handle the transition and the violence?"

He scoffed. "Like a duck to the water. He hated the Prajapatis intensely and wanted to wipe them away from the face of the earth. Most of my time went in trying to keep him out of trouble."

Anika frowned. "But he is friendly towards me."

"I know. I was surprised too."

Abhay told her about the construction of new units within the province that would keep Dev busy along with most of the Singham and Prajapati people.

It began to get dark outside.

"Do we have to leave?" she asked softly.

"Yes," he said with regret on his face. "It's not safe here for long. But I promise, we can come back here anytime you want to."

She smiled. "I'll be taking you up on that offer soon," she said.

Packing up everything, they headed home.

CHAPTER THIRTY

Anika was in the clinic checking some information on the computer when the phone rang. She answered the call with a silly smile on her face.

"Tonight. I'm taking you out for dinner. Be ready by six."

A month or so ago, if Abhay had said those words in that tone, she would have either been terrified or annoyed. But knowing what she did about him, she accepted the fact he wasn't the sweetly romantic type who whispered poetry or bought her flowers. For some reason, she had always thought she would be more attracted to a sensitive guy who wasn't afraid to show his feelings to the world. Surprisingly, she was more than happy with Abhay's private display of showing he cared.

"Hello, to you, too, Mr. Singham. Where are you taking me for dinner?"

"To the city. There is a good restaurant I know you'd enjoy."

Her heartbeat sped up. This was the first time after their marriage that she'd be stepping out of the Singham Estate. "Okay. I'll see what I can wear within my existing wardrobe."

"Six sharp, or I'm taking you out in your towel or whatever you are wearing at that time."

She laughed. "Okay. Okay. I'll be ready, Mr. Romantic."

There was a moment of silence. "Maybe I'd actually prefer if you were in your towel at six," he said in a husky tone.

She laughed again. Ever since she had lost her virginity to him at the lakehouse a few weeks ago, it almost felt like the gates to the dam were opened. He couldn't seem to keep his hands off her whenever he came home.

She felt the same way. The fact that he was willing to take a break from their marathon and take her out for dinner melted her heart. "I'll be waiting downstairs, Mr. Singham. You'll have to pick me up for a date from the doorstep, not the bedroom."

"We'll see—" He broke off in mid-sentence, and she could hear another man speaking to him. She couldn't hear what was being said, but the tone seemed urgent. "Anika, I've got to go. I'll come home soon. Bye." The call ended abruptly.

Placing the phone down, she continued with the experiment while excitement about their upcoming date made her work faster.

Her computer beeped, and her face lit up seeing the computer screen.

Unknown: *All good.*

Unknown: *Going off the grid as a precaution.*

Anika let out a deep sigh. *Her life was finally turning around.*

*****

Two hours later, thirty minutes before six o'clock, she was still struggling with what to wear.

She had never been on a proper date before. Sure, she had been on friendly dates with a close acquaintance or even some of her classmates, but never on a romantic date. She didn't know whether she should dress up to seduce or dress down casually. Abhay hadn't given her enough information of what kind of place he would be taking her to. Apart from 'you will enjoy it' and that the restaurant was in the city, she had nothing.

Jeans might make her underdressed if they were to go to a fancy place. A cocktail dress might be too much for a simple unassuming place with good food. So taking a wild guess, she picked a simple calf-length skirt with a top that had ethnic work within. It wasn't too dressy or casual.

The entire household was excited as she headed down the stairs. Malini let out a low whistle. She smiled at everyone who gave her approving nods and cheerful grins. The only person who was scowling at her was her husband.

As soon as she reached the bottom of the stairs, he leaned towards her and spoke softly. "I already regret this date. I rather stay up in our suite for the rest of the night."

She raised an eyebrow. "Mr. Singham, you promised me a date, and I'm holding you to that promise."

He swept his eyes over her body with an intense look. "You look... nice."

"Oh, thank you, you don't look too bad yourself." She laughed realizing it was his way of giving her a compliment.

He led her to a sleek sedan sports car.

"Are you driving us there?" He always took a driver and a bodyguard whenever he had gone out.

"It's a date," he said simply before closing the door and walking to the other side.

She smiled running her palm over his thigh.

"I'm barely hanging on by the thread as it is. If you touch me like that, I'm going to pull over and take you right here in the car while my security wonders what we are doing."

"Okay, no touching when you are driving. I get it." She laughed turning to look at the four cars following them.

"Keep your hands to yourself, Dr. Singham. We'll pick this up when we get back."

"Or we can spend the night wherever we are going?"

"No, it's not safe."

"I see."

He turned towards her for a brief second and saw the disappointed look on her face. "I know you'd rather have this date end the way we both want, Anika, but I can't take a risk with your security."

She sighed. "I understand." She leaned over to plant a kiss on his cheek. "Are you going to tell me where we are going?"

"A surprise."

She was quiet with a smile on her face.

When she didn't say anything, he turned to look at her briefly. "Why are you looking at me like that?".

"Because I have every right to do so. You are my husband, and I think I find you... cute."

"Cute?"

"Yes, I find you cute sometimes, Mr. Singham."

She laughed at his expression.

Two hours later, he pulled in front of a lavish hotel entrance. He held the door open as she got out of the car. He placed his arm around her waist, pulling her closer as they walked through the massive entryway of the hotel towards the restaurant.

Just as they were being directed to their table, she heard a man's voice calling. "Mr. Singham."

"Dr. Mani," Abhay turned to walk to a table to the far right and pulled Anika with him.

"Good to see you, Mr. Singham. What a pleasant surprise." The man looked to be in his forties.

"Anika, this is Dr. Mani. Dr. Mani, this is my wife." Abhay smiled politely.

"Oh, Dr. Singham. It is my pleasure to meet you. Mr. Singham and I discussed how to scale your online treatment model. Nice work you have done in a short time."

She was surprised Abhay had discussed her approach with someone else and hadn't dismissed it as nothing. "Thank you! We can use all the help we can get."

"Absolutely!" said Dr. Mani.. "I won't keep you longer. Please continue."

"Thank you." She shook Dr. Mani's hand with a smile and then let Abhay lead her to their table.

"I'm starving. What's good at this place." She asked eagerly as she looked at the menu.

"Let' get drinks first," he said as he put the drinks menu in front of her.

"Ohh. Are your trying to get me drunk Mr. Singham?" she asked in a coy tone.

He smiled. "Maybe."

She laughed and began checking the menu. When she made up her mind, she looked up from the menu, and realized Abhay was watching her with a tensed look.

Frowning, she realized he was not watching her, but something behind her. She turned and saw Ravi making some kind of gestures from the entrance.

"We need to leave, now," he stated, getting up quickly, and taking her by her arm.

"Abhay, is everything okay?"

"No, we need to get out of here." He led her through the back door and avoided the entrance.

"Your car?"

"Just keep walking." He instructed, making her break into a run in her heels.

She wasn't sure of what was happening, but something about Abhay's tensed look made her follow his instructions.

They walked through the restaurant kitchen with Ravi following her.

"Where is he?" Abhay asked in a chilling voice.

"Right outside the door."

"Bring my car around." He tossed his car key to Ravi, before holding her hand again and pulling her along. He pushed open the double doors and all his men who had followed them in the other cars were standing together.

"Who threatened my wife?" He demanded softly, walking towards the center of the group. She watched as he led her past his men towards a man who was on his knees tied up and beaten badly.

"Singham, please." The man's voice was barely audible.

"Who sent you?" Abhay asked again.

The man shook his head.

"Last chance. Give me the name."

The man continued shaking his head.

"Who?" Abhay kicked the man in his stomach.

The man screamed and then coughed, but did not speak.

Ravi handed Abhay a long butcher knife. "Who?"

There was visible fear in the injured man's face, but he still kept shaking his head. "If I tell you, I'm a dead man anyway."

"Your death will serve as a reminder for anyone who even thinks about hurting my wife." he snarled as he slit through the man's throat.

Anika gasped at the bloody sight in front of her but did not move.

She looked at Abhay after he kicked the dying man away from him and turned to look at her. He looked the same as he always did. So far she had seen him kill twice and both the times, he hadn't shown any reaction on his face. He was like a cold monster, devoid of any soft emotions when he took a life.

"Let's go," he said, wiping away the blood on his hands to a piece of cloth handed over to him.

The car was bought closer and they got in without another word.

She looked at him as he drove them back. His jaw was clenched and there was a tense silence in the car.

Slowly, she loosened her seatbelt and leaned towards him.

She kissed him softly on his cheek and laid a comforting hand on his lap. She spent rest of the journey leaning her head against his shoulder as he drove in silence.

There was only one thought that ran through her mind repeatedly that night.

He maybe a monster, but he was her monster, and she loved him...

CHAPTER THIRTY-ONE

Over the next few days, Abhay tightened the security further. He gave orders to people living in the estate to watch out for any suspicious happenings. Anika didn't press him for another date in the city, instead, she packed meals for them that they had within the estate premises. Apart from the lakehouse, there were plenty of other beautiful picturesque and peaceful locations where they could spend time alone and speak freely to one another.

Anika made it a point to read Devasena's journals each evening while waiting for Abhay.

"As a mother, I was accepting of my son's wishes to go against the traditions and follow his heart. But today, as a woman, I'm proud of my son, for going against the norms and marrying the woman he loved, even after what had transpired."

Through Devasena's eyes, Anika read about Vijay Singham's and Arundhati's marriage, and then about the violence that had taken place during the wedding. Anika's heart broke along with Arundhati's when Abhimanyu Singham was killed during the wedding.

She also read about how Devasena had made Vijay Singham promise her to take his pregnant wife away from the Singham Estate and also to a different country.

Devasena had written about how over the next ten years, the Prajapatis continued to harbor a grudge for the slight offered towards Neelambari. They kept instigating violence that led the people from the Singham province to first defend and then actively take part in it by attacking back.

She had tried to calm the Singhams as much as possible, but still a few of them felt they had to do it for the Singhams' honor.

Devasena's journals ended the day before the temple massacre—that killed Abhay's parents and Anika's father—had happened.

The last entry said, *"Today is the day when my Ajay's long-held wish will come true."*

It was the day when Prajapatis and Singhams were to meet to discuss the wedding proposal between Neelambari Prajapati and Ajay Singham.

*****

Anika was upset and felt foolish for feeling that way about something that had happened many years ago. Abhay distracted her in many ways. He made passionate love or sometimes sweet love, but he always ended it by making her feel wanted and cherished. He convinced her in every way that he was not going to let their family's past define their relationship.

Anika knew he was right, and she was determined to find happiness and work towards the marriage not only because Devasena had wanted it, but because she had fallen in love with Abhay Singham.

CHAPTER THIRTY-TWO

"Seventy rooms... in the house... and you... pick my clinic..." Anika panted the words. She was on top of Abhay who was lying on the cold sterile clinic floor.

His fingers dug into her hips as he pushed her harder and deeper on top of him, until they both groaned.

"Abhay... people might be waiting outside..." she gasped, even as she dug her nails into his chest and grinded.

He groaned and his movements became frantic. "No one will dare... they saw me come here..."

Anika was horrified that people knew what they were doing in the clinic. Her devil of a husband had a wicked grin. She tried to muffle her screams of ecstasy within his neck, but he didn't have any qualms. He let out a loud roar of release that she was sure could be heard outside.

"Oh God," she said, burrowing even more into his neck. "I'm not stepping out of this clinic. Everyone must have heard us!"

Abhay's chest shook in laughter. "Relax. Everyone is busy at the house with the preparations for the ceremony."

She raised her head. "But the ceremony is tomorrow."

"Yes, but usually they start the preparations a day ahead, so the house is going to be crowded with much activity. We have more privacy here."

She sighed and hugged him closer as he ran his fingers gently on her back.

After a few minutes, she stirred on top of him. "We should head back. This is my first event as a hostess. I want to be there when the guests arrive."

"You'll do fine. And everyone working here knows what needs to be done," he said.

They lay quietly for a while longer until they heard a faint cheering coming from outside.

"What's that?" she asked.

"Dev must have gotten here. There are organized fights that happen as part of the celebrations."

"Oh. I don't want to miss anything. Let's go check it out," she said.

She got up and began dressing while he watched her lazily with his head propped on one of his arms.

"Abhay, we need to join everyone," she said, even as her heart flipped watching his lazy smile and his naked body.

"Are you sure you want to leave this place, and not stay here for some more time?" he asked huskily.

"Yes," she said, with great difficulty, her voice coming out equally husky.

Abhay got up laughing and began putting on his clothes. As soon as they stepped out of the clinic, the cheering noise was louder.

As they walked towards the growing sound, Anika could see a crowd gathered around something.

"You have got to be kidding me!" Abhay scowled.

"What is it?"

"I see Prajapatis, too. My idiot brother must be challenging one of them to a fight."

A few of the Singhams spied Abhay and immediately gave way, until she walked along with him to front of the circle.

"Fuck!"

Anika didn't react to Abhay's crude word. She was too stunned at the sight in front of her.

Dev Singham was stripped down to a piece of long silk loincloth that showcased his immense muscles. He towered over his opponent by almost a foot.

Standing in front of Dev—was Sabitha. Dressed in cotton trousers and a tight tank top, with her long hair braided as usual, her cousin had a stony yet challenging look in her eyes.

"Oh my God. Is Dev seriously considering fighting Sabitha?" Anika asked.

There was a grim look on Abhay's face, but he didn't do anything to stop them.

"Abhay, do something! He's going to hurt her."

"I can't. That would only add insult to the Prajapatis," Abhay replied.

"But—"

"Don't worry. My bet is on your cousin. She is a natural. My brother might be a trained fighter, but his arrogance and temper will get the best of him during this particular fight."

There was a loud ring of a bell indicating that the fight could start. With bated breath, Anika watched it with disbelief.

Dev didn't move immediately. Sabitha used that chance to punch him on his face in a quick move before bouncing away from him. Dev's head snapped back with his jaw clenched as he watched Sabitha bouncing on her feet back and forth waiting for the next move.

"What's the matter, Singham, running scared already?" Sabitha taunted. She cracked her neck and indicated to him with her palms. "Come on, move that pretty ass."

Dev's biceps flexed indicating the anger and tension in his body. "No. I paused to ask you if you are sure about this. Because when it comes to you, I don't think I can hold back."

Sabitha smirked. "Or maybe, you are just scared that once and for all, we'll all know who is the stronger one between us is. Your people will find out that you're just a privileged prick who is your brother's bitch."

There were audible gasps from the crowd.

Dev let out a snarl. "You are going to regret that."

Sabitha let out a rare sweet smile rolling her shoulders and preparing her stance.

This time without any hesitation, Dev attacked Sabitha with various boxing moves. Sabitha dodged most of them making Dev even more pissed. Both the fighters moved in a circle drawing loud cheers, until Sabitha used one of her legs to kick Dev on his shin.

He let out a roar and then charged. Sabitha neatly dogged him and smashed her elbow on his jaw. They kept going at it until Sabitha visibly landed more punches on Dev.

"That's it. No more consideration because you have boobs and an arse," Dev muttered under his breath and charged once again. This time, he used his superior strength to bring Sabitha down on the floor. They both went crashing with Dev on the top.

Anika could see Sabitha gasping for air appearing to be in distress. Before Anika could intervene, Dev loosened his grip to get up. The next instant, Sabitha moved rapidly, wrapping her legs around Dev's neck in a strange chokehold.

Dev tried to struggle out of the trap, but he couldn't. One of his hands lay trapped under Sabitha's body as she tightened her legs around his neck. Using his free hand, Dev tried to push Sabitha's body away, but his movements grew weak.

Anika knew Dev was going to pass out in a few moments due to lack of air. He was growing sluggish and his face had turned grayish in color.

However, a few seconds before he completely blacked out, Sabitha loosened the hold and kicked his limp body away before getting up to the loud raucous cheers from the Prajapatis. Dev lay on the ground coughing and gasping for air.

Anika looked at her husband. She couldn't tell whether he was pissed or not by what he had just witnessed. "Help Dev, Abhay."

"No. Let him deal with it."

Dev slowly got up from the ground and walked towards Sabitha, stopping only a few inches away from her, towering over her. His eyes displayed his anger even as his mouth twisted in a smirk. "Well, what can I say? The best man won. But don't you think this manly display would actually put my brother off rather than make him see you as a woman?" His eyes swept the length of her. "He's definitely not going to leave his beautiful and kind wife for someone like you," he taunted.

Anika was shocked at Dev's rude behavior. He was so charming albeit cocky with the women living in the Singham Estate. He was even friendly and pleasant towards her.

Sabitha didn't seem to be affected by any of his insults. "Don't worry, Singham. I already knew that." She smirked. "Growing up with a pretty man like you, I figured your brother would prefer a pretty wife, too." Sabitha's comeback drew laughs as she strode away from the makeshift arena towards the mansion.

"I'm going to talk to her," Anika told Abhay, before she began pushing through the crowd to reach her cousin. By the time she cleared out of the circle, Sabitha was gone.

Since the celebrations continued, Anika had the lunch delivered to her room. Abhay joined her for lunch and then went back to the celebration. She had wanted to join everyone as well, but she got 'summoned' by her aunt through one of her aunt's personal maids.

Anika headed towards the north wing of the house where her aunt was apparently waiting for her.

As she walked on the polished marble floors of the Singham Mansion, Anika couldn't help but notice the difference in her own feelings and behavior. She couldn't believe that it had only been a little over three months since she had been called from the United States under false pretenses and trapped by her aunt. She had been terrified and helpless then, but right now, she was waiting to have the confrontation with her aunt.

As soon as she received confirmation that Myra and her parents were taken to a safe house, everything changed. Neelambari Prajapati had no bargaining or rather blackmailing power over her anymore.

Anika's steps slowed down as she passed through a large balcony overlooking the makeshift fighting ring. There were sounds of cheers, and it was obvious that the fights were continuing since morning. What really made Anika pause were not the ongoing fights, but the woman who lay perched in the shadowed nook of the balcony wall.

Something about the way Sabitha sat watching the setting sun made Anika go towards her.

Sabitha looked incredibly lonely. Anika didn't know why, but even though she knew her cousin was fully capable of murder, she did not harbor any fear towards her. Maybe because she had learned from Abhay that sometimes to end violence, one needed to resort to violence.

"Sabitha?"

Her cousin jumped slightly at the interruption. She looked at her for a few seconds before turning back to the view outside. "What do you want?" Sabitha asked in a monotone.

"Are you okay?" Anika could see that Sabitha's split lip was visibly swollen at the corners.

"I'm fine," Sabitha replied still staring out.

"I can have some ice sent up to you. It will help with the swelling."

"No thanks. I think I'll live," Sabitha said dryly.

Anika couldn't help but notice how similar Abhay and Sabitha were in many things. Both led a group of violent factions and had to be brutal to instill fear and respect within the people. Dev was a Singham, too, but most of the time, he was a cocky sweet talker who got work done in a different way. He was quick to smile and laugh. Unlike him, Abhay and Sabitha were the silent kind who only resorted to dry humor on rare occasions.

Sabitha would have suited Abhay better when it came to picking a Prajapati as a Singham bride. Did Sabitha think so, too?

Her cousin was watching a fight between Abhay and Dev. There were laughter and cheers as the brothers grappled together using some traditional fighting moves.

There was no wistfulness in Sabitha's eyes, but then, like Abhay, her cousin wasn't exactly the demonstrative kind.

Anika gave in to the need to ask her cousin about something that had been burning inside her. "The night before my wedding, did you call for a meeting with Abhay to convince him to marry you instead?" She recalled listening to Dev and Abhay's conversation on her wedding night. And even during the fight this morning, Dev had made a snarky remark to Sabitha about impressing Abhay.

Sabitha tore her eyes away from the fight to look at Anika. She stared quietly for a few seconds. Anika thought she wouldn't get an answer, but surprisingly, she did.

"Yes. I had called for Abhay Singham the night before the wedding for the sole purpose of seducing him and convincing him to marry me instead."

Anika was stunned. "You are... in love with Abhay?" she asked.

Sabitha scoffed. "No. I don't love him or any other man. That kind of love is for fools," she said.

Anika didn't know what to think of her cousin's response.

A small smirk played on Sabitha's face. "I'm not here to try to seduce your husband away from you."

Anika shook her head. "I know that already. I'm just wondering about your motive back then."

Sabitha stilled for a couple of seconds before she shrugged. "Power, not a motive enough?"

This time it was Anika who took her time to analyze the enigma that was her cousin. "Maybe, but power wasn't the only thing driving you to want to marry Abhay. I think there must be something else that you wanted to accomplish."

Sabitha let out a half smile. "You are quite perceptive. Not the same frightened girl from three months ago."

Anika shrugged. "Well, three months ago I was held hostage, and my family was threatened. So, of course, I was terrified."

"And now?"

"Now, I know my family is safe, and that I'm no longer a hostage." Her chin rose slightly, involuntarily. "I'm here with Abhay, willingly."

Sabitha nodded briefly. "Glad you are not ill treated by any of the Singhams. One of the reasons why I thought it was a good idea to seduce Abhay Singham... was also to stop him from marrying you. I wasn't sure you would survive this place for long."

Anika was surprised. She didn't think Sabitha gave a damn about her. In fact, Sabitha had scared the shit out her during the stay at the Prajapati mansion.

Definitely there was more to everyone here than what met the eyes.

"Thank you," Anika said earnestly.

"Don't thank me. Like you said, I had other reasons, too, for wanting Singham's power."

The sun disappeared behind the horizon making it darker. "Our aunt is waiting to talk to me. Let me finish talking to her, and then I'll come get you for dinner. I noticed you didn't have lunch with us this afternoon."

Sabitha didn't respond.

Anika began to walk away. She stopped when heard Sabitha call her name.

"Anika."

She turned to look at Sabitha, but couldn't see her face within the shadows.

"Don't trust Neela with anything," her cousin said quietly.

"I wasn't going to. I know she's crazy with her beliefs of Singham bloodlines and drought and everything. She's probably going to re-iterate the same thing along with the same threats as before."

Sabitha laughed softly. Anika realized it was a bitter laugh. "Neela doesn't give a damn about anyone. The last thing she would do is worry about the people or the drought."

Anika was stunned. "Then why did she..." Her words drifted as her mind began to furiously process what she had observed about her aunt.

"Just be careful around her," Sabitha warned.

Anika nodded and continued walking towards the north wing, her mind completely preoccupied with what Sabitha had just revealed about her aunt.

The door was partly left open, and Anika slipped inside. She took a few steps towards the gallery where there was a large seating area, but the sight in front of her made her stop short.

Her aunt was standing very close to a wall with her face stuck to a large life-sized portrait, while running her fingers over it and murmuring something.

Anika's keen ears picked up the name her aunt murmured over and over again.

"Vijay..."

The portrait was of Vijay Singham, Abhay's father. The resemblance to Abhay was so uncanny that it was close to creepy seeing her aunt caressing the inanimate picture.

Anika cleared her throat making her aunt jump. "You asked for me?" she enquired politely.

Neelambari wiped her tears before turning. "Yes." She moved towards the seating area and sat on one of the chairs. "Sit," she pointed at an empty chair.

The fact that Neelambari was ordering her in her own house rubbed Anika the wrong way. "I prefer not to," she said quietly. "This room is only meant for Singhams. We receive guests in a different wing. Follow me," she said, walking away.

Anika didn't bother to check whether her aunt was following or not. The fact that the woman who had threatened her family with harm was present in the house boiled her blood.

One of the maids saw her heading towards the guest receiving room in the north wing and hurriedly opened the door.

"Thank you, Priya."

"You are welcome. Would you like anything to be sent up from the kitchen?"

"No, thanks." Anika looked over her shoulder. "My aunt will be leaving shortly. Inform her people and ask them to prepare for the journey."

Neelambari looked livid, but she didn't comment.

Anika continued inside the room and sat on the high-back winged hostess seat. "Do be seated." She pointed to the sofa opposite to her.

Her aunt strode towards it and sat down. There was a long stretch of silence where each woman sized up the other.

"I think becoming a Singham must have really gotten into your head, my dear niece."

Anika smiled. "Believe me, it didn't. If I were to behave like a true Singham, then anyone threatening my family would be lying dead in front of my feet not summoning me like a lackey."

Her aunt's body tensed up, and she visibly dug her nails into the soft leather of the couch. "Watch how you talk to me, girl. I'm still the one running this show."

Anika sat back. "Not anymore," she said confidently. "I'm sure your goons must have informed you by now about not being able to track my family."

Neelambari didn't reply. Her eyes flared with anger and a few moments later, her mouth spread into a smile. "So you managed to keep your family safe. Well done! But you know what? I really don't care about them anymore. You are already married, and from what I can see you are truly married with the possibility to provide the Singham heir. My mission is already accomplished."

Neelambari's smile and words churned inside Anika's stomach, but she kept a calm look on her face. "I don't think it's just the marriage and heir you were after."

"Oh?"

"There is something else. And I believe it has got to do with Vijay Singham."

For a brief moment, the look on her aunt's face indicated shock and panic. "What nonsense—"

"I've seen how you watch, Abhay. I've heard you call him Vijay several times."

"Because he looks like his father. I don't appreciate this—"

"I just saw you hugging Abhay's dead father's portrait."

"Listen to me, you—"

"You loved him. Yet you agreed to marry his brother. Why?"

"I agreed to marry a Singham for the sake of people."

"You don't give a damn about the people. I'm sure you had a selfish motive. This feud wasn't just because he broke off the engagement to marry someone else. There is more to it. And I'm determined to find out everything."

There was visible panic and outrage on Neelambari's face. Her entire body shook and trembled. "You will find out nothing!" she hissed.

"Oh, so there is something then," she stated, while her aunt's fingers dug into the soft leather of the couch.

"I will find out what it is, and I can promise you I will not rest until I do." Anika spoke those words calmly and in a matter-of-fact tone, making her aunt break into a sweat. She got up from her chair. "Don't ever call for me again. If I have anything to say to you, I'll send for you." With those final words, Anika strode out of the room, leaving her visibly upset and terrified aunt behind.

CHAPTER THIRTY-THREE

Anika returned to the festivities happening outside. An hour later, Neelambari, along with a small group, waited near the entry way of the Singham Mansion, for the cars to be brought.

Seeing Neelambari waiting out with her luggage, the atmosphere changed to that of a tension-filled one.

Anika strode towards her aunt. "I wish you had stayed longer," she said in a deliberately louder tone, to be heard by people around. "But it's so nice of you to allow your people to stay back and enjoy the festivities even though you prefer to go back and rest in the Prajapati Estate."

Neelambari remained quiet.

"I hope you get better. There is so much to catch up on, and so much more to know about you. I promise I will visit the Prajapati household soon."

Neelambari got into a car and stared ahead without acknowledging Anika or her words.

Soon the car drove away.

Anika smiled at the people around. "On behalf of the Singhams, I would like to welcome the Prajapatis to the Singham Estate. Please enjoy the celebrations and our hospitality."

There were wild cheers from the people, most of whom must have been half-drunk and their stomach's filled with the rich food that was prepared exclusively for the celebration the next day.

Anika felt a heavy masculine arm slip around her waist. "That was impressive. Can we have our own celebration right now, Dr. Singham?" her husband's deep voice whispered into her ear.

Smiling, she looked at him and let him lead her to their master suite where they continued with their own private celebrations.

*****

The next morning celebrations resumed. During the middle of the celebrations, Abhay made an announcement.

"We have obtained the necessary permissions to divert the Singhoor River towards the Singham-Prajapati border. The projects to dig in our canals will begin starting next week. There will also be three new factories that will be set up within our province."

Abhay looked at his brother and then at Sabitha.

"Dev and Sabitha will work with all of you to make these projects a success. We will make our lands prosperous again."

There were cheers all around, along with an anticipation of a better future.

Anika felt overwhelmed with the amount of pride she felt towards her husband.

Abhay Singham was a true leader.

CHAPTER THIRTY-FOUR

Anika was sitting in the library, reading a book when the phone rang.

She answered it with a smile on her face. "Dr. Singham here."

"Ann?"

She froze as she heard the familiar voice.

"Ann? Is that you?" the girl on the other end asked urgently.

"Myra..." Anika whispered as her eyes began to well up with tears.

"Oh my God, Ann. You are safe... you are safe!" There were sobs on the other end of the line causing her to break down as well. She couldn't control her crying of sheer relief as she heard her sister speak.

She wiped away her tears and took a deep calming breath. "Myra. How are you? How are Mom and Dad? And also Nathan," she asked urgently.

"We are all safe, Ann. We are only worried about you. We heard what happened."

"Don't worry about me, Myra. Just keep Mom and Dad safe until everything is sorted."

"Yes. We are still at a safe house, and Justin is working with the cops to remove the threat completely. They have already caught a couple of men and are questioning them."

Anika felt her mind at ease listening to her sister. "That's good. Last time I heard from Justin, he'd mentioned they would simply be deported to be tried at the Indian courts."

"Yes. Unfortunately that's the law," Myra grumbled.

As long as her family was safe, Anika didn't care where Neelambari's goons were tried by the law.

"How are you, Ann? We can't wait to have you back with us." Her sister sobbed.

Anika didn't know what to say to that. She had been insistently planning to get her family to safety from the day she had gained access to Abhay's computer. Planning her own escape, although not her priority then, she had always thought she'd eventually get back to her old life.

And now... she didn't want to go back.

"Ann?"

Taking a deep breath, she answered her sister. "I'll see you guys soon, Myra. I'll also be bringing Abhay... my husband."

There was silence.

"What are you saying, Ann. Aren't you planning to leave him and get back to us like you said?"

Anika shook her head even though she knew her sister couldn't see her. "No, Myra. I love him. Now that you guys are completely safe, I'm going to tell him everything—"

"Ann, stop with the madness." Her sister's voice shook in concern. "Is this the same man who forced you to marry him?" Myra asked.

Anika bit her lip. "Yes. But he had a reason—"

"Isn't this the same guy who kills people, and threatened to kill you as well, if you didn't listen to him?"

"No. No. That part was a misunderstanding—"

"What part, Ann? The killing people or threatening to kill you?" Myra asked in disbelief.

"Myra, listen to me. You don't understand—"

"Please Ann. I'm begging you..." Anika could hear Myra's sobs. "I don't know what those people did to you or how they influenced you. Please, come back."

"I'm going to come, Myra, I promise. But—"

"No. Right now, Ann. That's why I'm calling you. Justin has already made an escape plan. Pavan, his contact will be waiting for you at the Karnul railway junction. Board any of the passing trains there. Ravi will also have your flight tickets and a passport ready."

When Anika fell silent, listening to the plan, Myra began to panic. "Ann, promise me you are coming. Please."

Anika still didn't reply, her mind torn between her family and her newfound love.

"Ann, listen to me. You might be experiencing confusing thoughts about your captor. But please remember, at end of the day, he's still your captor. You might feel you love him, but in reality, none of what you are feeling is true. It's called a Stockholm Syndrome. Look it up!"

Myra was studying criminal psychology and knew what she was talking about. However, Anika didn't have to look up the meaning for that term. She already knew what it meant.

Her heart began to pound as her mind tried to process the next course of action and the various implications. "I'll be there," Anika whispered, before ending the call.

Over the next few minutes, she sat in the library staring blankly at the wall. Then closing her eyes, she took a deep shuddering breath before opening them again.

She went down the stairs and walked towards the large parking area located next to the driveway of the Singham Mansion. Her eyes were wide, and she moved as though in a trance.

Ravi who stood near one of the cars speaking with the other drivers spotted her and came towards her. "Anika, do you need any help?" he asked.

"Yes. I need to pick up a friend from the Karnul railway station. Can you drive me there?" Her voice came out as a whisper.

Ravi hesitated for a second before smiling. "Sure. Let me know which car we'll need. Is your friend coming with a lot of luggage?"

"No. Any car should be fine. But we have to go alone. We can't take anyone else with us."

Ravi froze.

"Please Ravi. I want you to follow this order of mine. It's urgent. Please make it happen."

Ravi looked torn, but eventually he nodded. "Come down to the east side entrance. I'll bring a car there," he said.

Heart thudding, Anika went past the busy household towards the east entrance which only had tall trees and overlooked endless stretches of barren land.

Soon, Ravi got a small car that obviously didn't belong to the Singhams. It was his personal car.

Pulling the door open, she sat next to him in the front seat.

Ravi began to drive her to the destination.

Anika remained silent. Ravi remained silent as well as though he sensed a different kind of mood in her that he usually didn't encounter.

Her eyes took in the familiar landscape outside as the car sped through.

I'm addicted. I'm so addicted to you that I don't think I can stay without having your taste on my tongue or your smell inside my lungs.

She suppressed a sob at the memory of his words.

She recalled how she woke up sometimes and found Abhay watching her with a look that made her feel like the most precious person in the world.

Memories of the time they spent together, and the conversations they had, bonding over their childhood adventures, and talking about things they hadn't told anyone else apart from each other ran through her mind.

Did it really matter how long it usually takes to fall in love?

She knew what she felt for her husband was real and worth fighting for. She also knew without doubt that Abhay felt the same way about her.

"Ravi."

"Yes, Anika," he responded with a grave voice.

"Please turn back. I don't want to go for my friend right now. I'll come back later... with Abhay."

Ravi nodded, and without saying anything else, he slowed the car down and reversed it and drove them back towards the Singham Estate.

Even though worry about her parents and sister remained, her heart felt much lighter with the decision she'd taken.

"I'm sorry, Ravi, for wasting your time."

"That's okay. I understand," he said gently.

Did he suspect she was trying to leave the Singham Estate? And if so, why didn't he say anything or call Abhay immediately? She felt touched by the loyalty and trust most of the Singhams showed her.

"Ravi... I..."

Whatever she was about to say was cut off when she was jerked hard within the seat as they crashed into another car. Their car spun in circles before coming to a halt. Before she could catch her breath and ask whether Ravi was fine, they were surrounded by more than a dozen SUVs.

CHAPTER THIRTY-FIVE

"The Senanis," Ravi said in a horrified whisper. And then he looked at her with widened eyes. "Please, remain here. I'll go speak with them and get this sorted. And no matter what happens, don't get out of the car."

Anika's heart was thumping loudly in fear. "It's not safe, Ravi. Don't get out. I'll go speak to them."

Ravi shook his head vehemently. "Please. Don't fight me on this. I've already sent out the code to Abhay and everyone else at home. Help should arrive shortly. Just—"

Before Ravi could finish, a loud thunking noise sounded on her side of the car. The door was being attacked by what appeared to be an axe. She knew the car was bulletproof, but had no idea how long it could withstand an axe.

There were at least twenty men surrounding the car watching them with wild eyes as though they couldn't wait to tear the car apart.

She was trembling as she tried to think of a way out.

Less than five minutes later, the entire car door on her side was wrenched apart, and she was being pulled out of the car.

Ravi tried to intervene, but a loud gunshot went off within the car.

"No! Don't kill him!" she shouted in panic as she saw Ravi's bleeding arm. "I'll come with you."

"That's good. Then don't trouble us and come out quietly," said one of the men.

With her heart pounding loudly in fear, she pushed herself out of the car. Immediately, hands grabbed her.

"Finally, we have the Prajapati whore with us," said a tall man who looked much more put together than the rest of the men. There were several snickers at the crude comment. "You kept us waiting for a very long time, sweetheart. That bastard Singham must have known that and kept you well guarded."

She remained quiet, trying not to show any visible fear. There was an evil grin on an otherwise a handsome face in front of her. "I lied. I hate all Singhams. And I especially hate leaving them alive," he said, before shooting into the car multiple times.

Anika screamed and struggled to go towards Ravi. "Let go! Let me go to him," she shouted.

She began to fight. She kicked, scratched, and clawed with her free hand while ignoring the pain on her other hand where the man held her in a bone-crushing grip. The man raised his hand and slammed into her face. Stars exploded behind her eyes followed by pain. Reeling and staggering, she tried to remain upright, refusing to give into the blackness.

A rough hand grasped her under her chin, forcing her to stare into the man's cold smiling eyes. "I'm going to have so much fun breaking you."

The man dragged her into one of the cars. Her head continued to reel from the blow, and it was getting hard to focus. She stopped struggling, but jerked at his grip. She tried opening the lock on the car door next to her, but the child locks were enabled.

She turned her head back to watch the abandoned car with Ravi inside moving further and further away. "I'm so sorry," she whispered with tears in her eyes. This was her fault. The Senanis killed Ravi because she put him in danger by asking him to help her escape.

Will Abhay find out what happened? He'll know she drove away to escape using the pretext of picking up a friend.

Will he hate her? Or mourn her?

She shook her head refusing to accept whatever was happening to her passively. The Senanis had no leverage on her.

"If you kill me, Abhay won't like that," she said confidently.

The man next to her barked out a laugh. "Oh, I'll be happy if he doesn't like it at all. But don't worry, I'm not going to kill you." His eyes roved over her face and body lingering on her chest. "I'll just fuck you and send you back to him."

She inhaled a sharp breath at the threat. "He'll come for me. You won't get the chance to send me back to him."

"Ah," he said. She recoiled as he ran his thumb over her lip. "Yes, definitely. With a face like this, especially the lips, he's going to come for you. Did he teach you how to suck a cock and make a man happy?" he asked with a leer.

She didn't open her mouth to answer, fearing he'd push his thumb inside her mouth. Instead, she stared stubbornly ahead until there was laughter from the man next to her.

He moved his thumb away. "Has Abhay Singham mentioned me to you?" he asked.

"No."

"Well, then let me introduce myself. I'm Hemant Senani, your future lover, and if you are lucky, the father of your child."

Her nails dug into the seats as anger and fear warred within her while snickers filled the car. The car kept taking them further and further away from the Singham lands.

*****

After what seemed to be an eternity, they stopped in front of a large warehouse, and the man dragged her into it, as she struggled.

Tears burned her eyes and all the emotion she'd kept bottled up inside exploded from her. "You are a fool! What the hell are you going to accomplish by this? More feud? Half of your people are already dead due to senseless violence and stupid ignorance. Stop this madness right now!"

"Shut up." The man said with rage in his eyes. "This is not senseless or ignorant. Our pride is our life, and if anyone dares to hurt that pride, they will have to pay with their lives." He dragged her closer. "Singhams' pride is in your dignity, which I'm going to enjoy stripping out of you."

Her heart pounded so hard she could barely breathe. She had to be smart and think of a way to stop that man from raping her, but she was clamming up as he ripped the material of her clothes.

He leaned forward, held her breasts, and pressed his body against her back grinding his erection against her. A wave of nausea rolled up her throat and she struggled to control it.

She felt his lips on her ears. "I'll show you what a real man feels like."

She heard the sound of his zipper, and then she began to struggle. It only excited him further. He brought out a sharp knife and began cutting through her clothes while the rest of the Senanis began to make lewd remarks.

His hands began to run up and down her sides making her skin crawl. She let her body go completely slack making him think she gave in. She turned her head back to look at him. He was nearly half a foot taller than her.

She threw her head back slightly baring her neck. Slowly, he relaxed his hold on her continuing to grind against her. Soon he took up the invitation, and she felt his lips on her neck.

The next minute, she bent her head down and reared, slamming her head back hard into his nose, until she saw stars once again. The man let out a roar, but before he could recover, she turned and slammed her heel into his bare crotch.

The man began to scream violently, and all the men drew out their weapons and pointed at her waiting for an instruction to kill her.

She closed her eyes shut, and thought of Abhay.

Her heart clenched at the thought of never having to see him or hold him again. She thought of her family and prayed that they'd all be okay even after she was gone.

Sounds of gunfire exploded around her, but her body didn't experience any pain. There were several screams, and then something sliced through her arm making her hiss out in pain. But the pain wasn't significant enough to drop her on the ground.

"Anika!" she heard someone calling her name.

She opened her eyes, thinking she was imagining Abhay's voice through the noises.

When she saw him standing a few feet away from her, she felt immense relief. He was shouting something at her, but everything around them was too loud for her to hear him. Her head was throbbing, and her ears continued ringing with the sound of gunfire.

There was so much blood around her, she didn't know which family it belonged to.

Abhay moved towards her, and she met him halfway.

He pushed her on the ground and covered her body with his. She could feel his movements as he lifted his hands and continued to shoot at people around him.

After the longest time, the gunfire stopped.

Everything was quiet, except for a wheezing noise made by a man lying a few feet away from her.

Abhay rolled away from her, and immediately her eyes fell on her tormenter, Hemant Senani.

Anika's heart began to thud. *Why was he kept alive?*

"Did this animal touch you?" Abhay asked quietly, his eyes on her torn clothes.

Anika couldn't get her tongue to function, so she nodded.

"Take this." Abhay extended his hand to give her a gun.

She hesitated.

Hemant Senani started to cough and spat out blood. His face was a bloody mess due to his broken nose. "I was having fun with your wife, Singham," he taunted. "A real hot little piece who likes it rough. Her cunt is still so tight, even though you must be regularly fucking her. Maybe that's why she couldn't get enough of me because I have a bigger cock."

Anika flinched while she felt conflicting emotions within her.

She did feel violated by the man in front of her who had every intention of raping her. He was also taunting her and Abhay.

But she couldn't take a life.

She clenched her hands, waiting for some kind of instincts to kick in. Natural instincts that will tell her whether or not to take a life.

"Take the gun, Anika," Abhay repeated with a dead calm tone.

"I-I can't," she said. "I can't kill someone."

"It's not just someone, Anika," he said in a rational tone. "It's a fucker who dared to touch you and is taunting you again. I'm giving you a chance to take your own revenge."

When she stood frozen, the man on the floor laughed. "You know why she's hesitating, Singham? Because she loved being fucked by a real man. Give her a choice, and she'll let me go. Right, sweetheart? We had fun didn't we? Loved how you sucked my cock. I'm looking forward to a lifetime of more fun with you."

"Anika!" Abhay snapped at her.

"Abhay..." she whispered, wanting to badly tell him no again, but something in his eyes stopped her.

Abhay looked at her with a calm look. "This man is yours to do what you want," he said. "But remember, whatever you choose, it'll be your choice for life."

Tears fell down her eyes as she trembled, staring at the gun. She understood what Abhay was doing. He had found out about her attempt to escape. He was giving her a choice between choosing to pick his way of life or return to her old life.

Anika closed her eyes and took a deep breath.

Then opening her eyes, she took the gun carefully from Abhay's hand and pointed it at the man on the floor.

The man leered. "Ah, is this the part where I'm supposed to be begging for my life?"

Leaning down, she placed the gun to the Senani man's head. And then taking another deep breath, she pulled the trigger.

CHAPTER THIRTY-SIX

She sat quietly next to Abhay as the car headed home. She was too exhausted, and there were too many emotions to process right then. So she didn't process any of them—she let herself stay numb and embraced the silence. She pulled his shirt closer around her breathing in his beautiful masculinity.

As soon as they reached home, she asked for Ravi's wife. "She's with him at the hospital in the city," Abhay replied gravely.

Her heart jumped with hope. "He's alive?"

He nodded. "Yes. They are operating on him, and we were told there is a chance he might make it."

Anika prayed fervently that he did. She felt another wave of guilt consume her.

"Let's go inside and talk," he said as he led them towards their suite. He wrapped his arm around her shielding her from curious and concerned glances.

She felt even guiltier seeing the worry on some of those faces.

As soon as they entered, he took her towards the bathroom. "Do you want a quick shower or a bath?" he asked. His voice was matter of fact while his face was devoid of any emotion, almost as though he knew she was hanging by a thread, and he had to be the one to take charge.

"Shower." She wanted to get the stench of blood and gunpowder away from her body.

Immediately, he began removing her clothes, but his touch was impersonal like that of a doctor. After she was completely bared of her clothes, he turned on the shower. "I'll be waiting in the other room if you need me," he said softly, before striding out.

He was almost at the door, when she whispered his name. "Abhay..."

He stopped, but he didn't turn. His shoulders were rigid, and his entire body was tensed.

"Please, don't leave. I need you," she said. When he slowly turned towards her with a face that held no expression, she stretched an arm. "I want you to help me forget that an animal held me. I feel so dirty inside and out."

Finally, there was an expression on his face.

Rage.

He strode towards her and he held her. "That animal is dead. You killed him, remember? Nothing can ever soil you. You will remain pure inside and out even if hundreds of such animals dared to touch you in any way."

She felt tears of gratitude well up in her eyes as she heard him. "I wasn't raped, Abhay. He was taunting you to think otherwise."

He hugged her close and his body shuddered in relief.

She pulled away from him and her shaking hands reached up to unfasten his clothes. Once she was done, he let her lead him into the shower.

Despite his anger and hurt, he gently began to soap her, and held her under the water, washing away the blood. She did the same with him, until the floor was clear of all traces of blood.

Turning off the shower, he grabbed a towel and dried them. He wrapped one around her and led her into the room towards the nook where food was placed. "You must be hungry. Eat before you rest," he advised.

She stopped and held his eyes. "I don't need food. I need you," she said softly.

When he didn't respond, she dropped the towel wrapped around her, and moved towards him. Then holding his face with a firm grip, she pulled him close and joined their lips together.

She kissed him with urgency, until she heard a growl emitting deep within him. He picked her up and took her towards their bed to lay her on top of it.

Before he could climb on top of her, she sat up and placed a hand on his chest. She pushed him.

He paused, scanning her face. Slowly, he lay next to her, pulling her on top of him.

She didn't wait for any preliminaries. She was more than ready. In fact, she needed this like it was her next breath of air.

She joined them together with a savageness that shocked her.

She moved over him with an aggression that began filling her entire body, consuming her, and making her feel alive.

She could see it in his eyes that he was similarly affected, but he let her lead.

Only when they found their first mutual releases, did he take over.

Not giving her enough time to even catch her breath, he flipped them over and he began to kiss her. He lingered over every bruise and kissed away the horrible moments of that day.

She let herself go as he repeatedly took her over to the edge, through the rest of the night.

CHAPTER THIRTY-SEVEN

The next morning when she woke up, he wasn't next to her.

Her eyes flew around the room and found him.

He was already dressed. And he was sitting on a chair facing the bed, watching her with steepled fingers.

"Abhay..." She called out his name, hoping to have him greet her the same way as the last few weeks.

She refused to recall the previous day's events. She wanted them gone permanently from her memory.

"Abhay," she said again with a small smile.

He didn't return it.

"Why didn't you tell me everything about your family?" he asked instead.

Her smile disappeared. She was feeling regret about the same thing. But before she could say anything, he asked her the question she had been dreading the most.

"Did you really have any intention of asking your parents or sister to visit you here?"

She took a shuddering breath before answering him with truth. "No... I didn't want them involved in this world."

He flinched ever so slightly. "I see."

Even though it wasn't obvious, she saw the hurt look on his face, and went closer to him. "Abhay that was much before. I was worried for their safety and didn't want to take any chances then."

He looked at her quietly. "You don't have to worry about your family anymore. I've contacted your aunt this morning and warned her clearly. I told her if I saw a Prajapati anywhere close to your family or friends, it would end badly for them."

Before she could thank him and feel immense relief, he continued speaking in a monotone that worried her. "I've also contacted a few people in San Francisco. They will provide protection for you and your family, until you are all completely at ease."

Her heart stopped. "What do you mean protection to me in San Francisco?"

He didn't reply immediately.

"I think it's best if you go back to your life. You don't belong here. This violence, and the feud, it might continue for decades and a few more generations together."

She shook her head. "No! You gave me a choice last night. And I made it already. I want to be here with you."

She could see a flash of regret passing on his face. "I know. I shouldn't have made you take a life."

Panic raced through her body as she went towards him. "I don't care that I killed that man. He deserved it. I want you to stop trying to push me away."

"The man you were supposed to meet yesterday is downstairs waiting for you. He will accompany you to the States where the rest of your family is waiting for you."

"Abhay, stop."

"Anika, what we had between us was good, but it's over now. I can't risk your life anymore. And neither can I cage you to keep you safe. You felt that way, too, yesterday. So please... go. Go back to your family."

"I love you!" she shouted in a frantic tone. She saw him flinch. "I want to be with you, Abhay. Don't push me away!"

He looked at her calmly. "My life is dedicated to my people. You already know I can't stop doing what I can to bring peace to this land. Please don't make this hard for both of us."

Her lips trembled as she heard his words of rejection. "Please..." she begged collapsing on her knees in front of him.

Taking a deep breath, he held her face gently and then, he let go, and walked out of the room and also her life.

CHAPTER THIRTY-EIGHT

"Anika?"

A man's voice sliced through her concentration. Anika looked towards the door at Nathan who was watching her with concern on his face.

"It's almost eight, Anika. You even skipped lunch. You only ate fruit all day. I grabbed a quick dinner for you in case you are too tired to stop somewhere or cook."

Anika nodded. "Thanks, Nathan." She mechanically placed the food next to her.

She went back to her work, but Nathan remained standing. "Do you need a ride home tonight? You look really tired. You've been working nearly fifteen hours each day the last two weeks."

Anika threw him a small smile. "No, I'm good. You know I need to get this done tonight."

"I know," he said. There was sadness in his voice. "I'll see you tomorrow then? At your place around noon?"

"Yup."

"I'll pick up something for lunch," he offered.

"No need. I'll order in for us."

He nodded and left her office.

Anika continued to work the rest of the night until she could finally wrap up and called it a day.

As soon as she entered her apartment, her eyes fell on the blinking red light of the phone. She rushed towards it and played the messages.

"Anika, Dad and I are coming at nine. Let me know if you want me to bring something."

She played the next message.

"Ann, Mom is trying to reach you. As usual, she is harassing me when she isn't able to get hold of you." There was laughter in her sister's voice. *"Anyway, Justin and I will come to your place at eleven. We are bringing lunch, so don't bother cooking or picking up anything."*

There were no other messages since that morning when she had last heard them.

Anika felt a keen disappointment and also anger. She furiously wiped her tears away and went towards her bedroom to change. She had to catch some sleep before she prepared to spend the day with her family and Nathan.

*****

The next morning she woke up at eight and began to get ready for the day. She caught the sight of her reflection while she stood in front of the vanity mirror about to throw on some makeup.

Her face looked pale and gaunt with dark circles around her eyes. She had lost a significant amount of weight over the last two weeks. She barely ate, and what little food she tried to eat, didn't sit well.

She tried to cover up the dark circles with concealer to avoid the worried fussing from her mom. Just as she was about to put the finishing touches, she heard the doorbell ring.

She straightened her dress that flattered her rather than show how much weight she had lost. Then giving herself one final look, she went towards the door.

Hurriedly, she dragged the door open with a welcoming smile. Her smile froze.

Standing in front of her looking larger than life was her husband.

"May I come in?" he asked while his eyes swept over her face taking in each and every detail.

Anger rushed through her when she saw worry written on his face. She stepped aside to let him in and closed the door shut.

"Anika, how are you—"

She swung her arm and slapped him. His face whipped to the side with the force of it.

Slowly he turned towards her again. "Anika—"

She slapped him on his other cheek with an equal amount of force.

When his head drew back towards her, his eyes were flared. "Anika listen—"

She raised her hand to slap once again, but this time he held her hand. He pulled the other free hand as well and held her close. She began hissing and struggling.

"Can you stop and listen for a minute!" he demanded.

"You pushed me away!" she shouted into his face. "I begged, but you still threw me out!"

He flinched. "I know. I'm sorry."

"Screw your sorry and shove it up your ass!" she hissed.

She saw the shock on his face at her crude words.

He blanked his expression, before trying once again. "I'm sorry—"

She began struggling once again. "I told you I don't want your shitty sorry." She leaned down and bit his hand.

He didn't let her go. He growled, and then picked her up to push her against the wall before kissing her hard. She struggled against him letting out angry muffled noises as he continued to kiss her.

She bit him, but he still didn't let go. He kept kissing until her mouth softened, and she began kissing him back.

He finally pulled away when she went completely silent. He wiped away the tears she didn't realize she had shed during their kiss.

"You sent me away," she whispered through a blur as more tears welled up in her eyes.

"I know," he replied softly. This time he didn't add that he was sorry. "I won't do it again," he said instead.

"Oh God, Abhay! I missed you—"

The doorbell rang loudly, interrupting their reunion.

Abhay frowned. "Are you expecting someone?" he asked.

"Yes. My parents, Myra, and Nathan."

"I see."

She slowly smiled. "No, you don't," she said, before moving away from him and wiping away the remnant tears from her face and answering the door.

"Anika! My baby!" Her petite mom pulled her towards her to hug her and held her in a death grip.

"Subadra, you'll choke our daughter. Let her lose, will you." Her stepdad laughed in amusement.

"My baby is leaving me, Jignesh Patel!"

Her mom held her hand and strode into the house and abruptly stopped short.

Anika's parents stared at the tall, elegantly dressed muscular man waiting in their daughter's living room. Anika's mom's eyes kept swinging between the man's impassive face to her daughter's. As soon as she saw the tear tracks on Anika's face along with the now visible dark circles, her eyes narrowed.

"Mom... easy," said Anika, letting out a laugh.

"So... you are Abhay Singham..." Her mom's voice drawled.

Anika was both amused and horrified listening to her mom speaking to Abhay in that tone. Back in Singham Estate, he was treated like an undisputable god. He laid down the law, and he was the law, but right here, he had to first deal with an angry wife and then an angry mother-in-law who was ready to scratch his eyes out for daring to make her precious daughter cry.

"Yes, Mrs. Patel. I am Anika's husband," he answered politely using his crisp British accent.

Her mom's expression flickered.

Anika stifled another laugh. She knew her mom was a sucker for British accents. During her childhood, Myra and she were forced to watch hundreds of romantic movies with British actors. One of the reasons why Yashwant Prajapati was able to sweep her mother away within months of meeting her was due to his British accent acquired during his studies in London.

"But... I was told that you live in a brutal place where there are no laws..." Her mom's words were hesitant.

Abhay's handsome face was still impassive. "Yes, Mrs. Patel. What you were told is all true."

Her mother shook her head slightly and took a deep breath. "Why are you here, Mr. Singham?"

Abhay's eyes fell on his Anika. "Please, call me Abhay. And I'm here to take my wife home. That is, if she'll have me back."

Anika's mother frowned and looked confused. "But she—"

"Mom," Anika interrupted her mother, still keeping her eyes on Abhay.

"Why should I come back?" she asked him softly. "What's stopping you from sending me away again? Everything is still the same back home."

Abhay eyes flickered with emotion. "I know, but I can promise you that I'll do everything to keep you safe."

Anika's face softened. "I don't need you to always protect me, Abhay. I know how to take care of myself."

"I know that. That's why I want you back, and also because I'm selfish enough to always want you with me."

"Why?" she asked.

He took a deep breath, and let his face show what he felt. "Because without you... it feels as though I'm not living. I'm simply surviving. I need my life back."

Tears freely ran down from Anika's eyes as she heard those words from her usually gruff husband.

"Go kiss him, you fool," her mother's obviously choked-up voice snapped.

Laughing softly, Anika ran to Abhay and crashed into him in a hug. She cried out all the loneliness she had felt during their separation. He held her gently, running his hand down her hair comforting her.

Soon, the rest of the guests arrived, and Anika introduced Abhay to everyone.

Myra mouthed a silent "wow" to her when she saw and spoke with Abhay with awe on her face. Anika laughed and felt happy and excited to show Abhay a part of her life.

"So, when can we visit the Singham Estate?" Myra asked Abhay during lunch.

"Anytime. Let me know a few days before, so we can prepare for your arrival."

Anika helped herself to more food. She was suddenly ravenous. All of her nausea seemed to have disappeared that day. "The three of us will try and fly to San Francisco as often as we can."

"Three? You mean with Dev?" Abhay asked.

Everyone seemingly froze around the table. All the eyes were on Anika who was slowly turning red. "Uh... Abhay. Can we speak privately for a minute?" she asked.

Abhay frowned when he saw the strange yet tensed faces around the table. He noticed there wasn't a negative tension—it appeared to be more because of anticipation.

Anika pushed her chair back and got up. She held his hand and took him inside to her bedroom. The bed badly tested his patience, but he held himself back when he saw the anxious face of his wife.

"What's the matter, Anika?" he asked.

Looking into his eyes, she took a deep breath and held his hands. "I'm pregnant."

He was stunned. He stared at her unable to work out any words.

Anika looked amused. "Say something, Abhay."

"How?" he asked, still in shock.

She let out a giggle. "Umm... the usual way, Mr. Singham. If I recall, you are incredibly good at the process of procreation."

Her face softened as wonder began to take over his face. "It probably was at the lakehouse."

"But you used protection.."

She smiled once again. "They are not hundred percent foolproof. And you must have really good swimmers to be able to get past the various protections we used."

Abhay shook his head, and finally a savage, possessive smile broke on his face causing Anika's heart to thud in excitement.

"You are completely mine now!" he growled and swept her off her feet to kiss her passionately. Later, when they pulled away to gasp in some much needed air, he continued watching her with the possessive look. "No force on earth can keep you away from me. Not even you!"

"Settle down, Mr. Caveman," she groaned out a laugh, squirming within her husband's arms.

"I can't," he said as he placed her gently on her bed. "I mean what I just said. You and our little one are my entire life from now on." He rained slow kisses on her face and then moved down her body until he held her still flat stomach. He kissed her belly gently before moving up with a vulnerable look in his eyes.

"I know you and our child can easily live without me. But please, choose me, and my life, even though your world might be a more suitable place to bring up children."

Anika sat on up her bed, running her fingers through Abhay's hair as he lay his head on her lap. "I was planning on chasing you to Singham Estate, and stay there whether you wanted me or not."

His head snapped up, and he looked at her in disbelief.

She smiled. "I resigned from my job. Yesterday was my last day. I told everyone I would be taking some distant courses in hospital management because I will be running a hospital in India." She leaned forward to kiss him on his lips. "My friends and family are here to say goodbye. I was planning on flying out in two more days. I even packed up whatever I needed." She pointed with her chin towards the suitcases standing against the wall.

A smile broke on his face. He moved up and pushed her back to bed, before climbing on top of her and kissing her deeply.

She felt his arousal and groaned into his mouth as her body responded violently due to their long separation.

"If I can't be inside you soon, I'm going to go mad," he growled.

"I know. But my parents..."

He exhaled noisily and dragged himself away from her. He lay on the bed next to her bringing his body under control.

She wrapped her arms around her body and shuddered feeling the need running through her. "Let's go out now. We are almost done with lunch, and they'll leave soon."

She dragged herself up and went towards the bedroom door and opened it. Giving him a hot sweeping look that flared his eyes, she strode out.

"Everything okay?" her mom asked.

"Yes."

"Where's Abhay?"

"He... uh... is still too overwhelmed with the news. He's going to join us shortly."

A couple of minues later, Abhay joined everyone looking calm and collected.

Everyone congratulated him.

"Thank you," he replied.

Soon, Nathan left and then Anika's parents.

"Hmm... you know what?" said Myra with a thoughtful look. "I think Justin and I are going to hang out for a bit longer. It's so much fun hanging out with you guys." Then she stared at Anika's frozen look and Abhay's impassive expression and burst out laughing.

"What? Not even a polite, *sure, please stay longer, lil sis*?" Myra giggled. Justin shook his head and dragged Myra out of the house.

As soon as Anika closed the door, Abhay swept her into his arms, and in record time had her deposited on her bed and stripped them out of their clothes.

"Did you miss me, Mr. Singham?" she asked breathlessly, staring at him in eager anticipation.

He dragged her up on the bed and covered her body balancing his weight on his arms and stared down at her with a desperate, hungry look. "You have no bloody idea how much, Dr. Singham."

Those were the only sentences they spoke for a very long time.

CHAPTER THIRTY-NINE

"Sir, can you please raise your chin a little? I'd like to capture that powerful jaw."

Abhay scowled at the portrait artist.

"Sir, although your scowl is pretty sexy, I think your wife will want you to appear happy in this family portrait."

Anika let out a muffled giggle. Abhay turned to frown at her, but seeing his wife's beautiful face with amusement dancing in her eyes, his scowl softened to a sheepish smile.

"I know you are dying to get the hell out of here," she said.

"Of course, I am. If it's really a portrait you need, then you should know that I could commission a portrait from one of the world's best artists. They will come to the Singham Estate and stay with us and work on the portrait based on *our* schedule." He was still outraged that they had to wait for another couple to finish up before them.

She smiled. "I know, but this one will always remain special to me," she said softly.

Abhay felt the familiar tug in his heart. He knew how much the day meant to her. They were exploring San Francisco as carefree tourists. The next day, he would be taking her back to Singham Estate where reality would catch up with them.

"Sir, please look straight ahead."

The portrait artist's voice intruded his thoughts, and he went back to scowling at the lady. His eyes wandered to the tourists walking on the opposite side of the road—some of them were laughing and clicking pictures.

His eyes fell on a man who was obviously from Indian origin. He looked familiar, especially with the way he grew out his beard and mustache and also the distinctive green and red colored tattoos on the neck. The man was facing his profile towards Abhay, so his tattoo couldn't be seen clearly. He was talking on the phone gesturing with his hands.

A couple of minutes later, he ended the call and looked straight ahead, raising his arm as though to flag a taxi. Their eyes met, and Abhay couldn't tear his eyes off the puckered flesh that covered the man's right cheek.

Everything froze as Abhay tried to process what he was seeing. Even the man's eyes widened, and he looked terrified.

Abhay got up from the bench slowly and watched as the man's lips kept uttering the same words over and over again.

Vijay Singham.

"Abhay?" Anika called out to him.

"Don't move. Stay right here. I'll be right back," he said and moved towards the man with purpose.

The man saw him coming towards him and began to walk away quickly.

Abhay didn't care for the oncoming traffic or the pedestrian rules and began to cross the road.

The man kept turning back looking frantically as he walked away. Soon he reached a taxi and wrenched opened the door.

Abhay ran faster. "Stop!"

The man stuck his head out of the taxi and frantically spoke with the driver. When Abhay was barely ten feet away from the car, it slid into the traffic and drove away.

He stood there, frozen and watching the taxi as it disappeared.

"Abhay? What happened? Who was that?"

He turned slowly and stared at his wife's worried look. "I think that was Narasimha Raidu, my father's bodyguard."

Anika frowned. "He moved to the States after the incident at the temple happened?"

Abhay simply stared at his wife as she stood with their cheap-framed portrait.

"Abhay, you are scaring me. Tell me what's wrong?" she demanded.

He took a deep breath, trying to sort out his thoughts. "Narasimha Raidu was supposed to have died in that fire along with our fathers. He was supposed to have died protecting my mother and father."

Anika looked stunned. "What?"

He tried to recall the sequence of the events that had apparently transpired on that fateful day, but each version based on who was narrating it, ended up being different.

"How are you so sure he was Narasimha Raidu?" Anika's calm voice tore through his musings.

"He looked at me in fear. And he called me Vijay Singham. He also had the Senani tattoo that belonged to his father's side of the family."

She was quiet as she took in the details. "So he faked his death for some reason. He was scared of your father?"

Abhay shook his head. "No, they grew up together. He even had a family. Malini is his daughter."

Anika was shocked. "Malini told me her father died in the fire as well. So he hasn't told anyone in his family, too."

They were silent, lost in their own thoughts.

"Maybe he was ashamed of not being able to protect the people he was hired to and also for being the only survivor. So he escaped." Even as Anika spoke those words, something didn't ring true.

Abhay took a deep breath. He held Anika's shoulders gently. "We'll have to postpone our tickets. I can't go back without finding that man," he said.

Anika nodded. "I'm fine, Abhay. I want to know what happened, too."

Abhay pulled out his phone and dialed. The phone began ringing, and it was answered after several rings. "Hello," a gruff deep voice answered.

"Dev, I'll be staying here with Anika for a few more days. I don't know for how long. I want you to handle things at the Estate."

"What happened?" Dev asked, sensing something.

"I think I saw Narasimha Raidu."

"What the fuck? Dad's bodyguard?" Dev almost shouted.

"Yes."

"I want to be there as well to hunt for that bastard and find out what happened."

"People need you there, Dev. Stay and handle everything while I look for him here."

There was silence. Abhay knew his brother well. Dev was mentally trying to check who could handle things while he flew in to join the hunt.

"Dev, stay. There are too many things happening at the Estate. Things are slowly falling into place with the canal and the units. We can't afford to mess up anything at this point."

There was another long stretch of silence, and then, "Fine," came out a grudging reply.

Ending the call, he looked at his wife. She had a determined look on her face as she began typing on her phone. "Let's start listing down contacts that can help us find that person."

The End.